DOCTOR WHO
MYSTERIOUS PLANET

DOCTOR WHO
MYSTERIOUS PLANET

Based on the BBC television series by Robert Holmes by arrangement with BBC Books, a division of BBC Enterprises Ltd

TERRANCE DICKS

Number 126 in the
Doctor Who Library

TARGET

A TARGET BOOK
published by
the Paperback Division of
W.H. ALLEN & Co. Plc

A Target Book
Published in 1988
By the Paperback Division of
W.H. Allen & Co. Plc
44 Hill Street, London W1X 8LB

First published in Great Britain by
W.H. Allen & Co. Plc 1987

Novelisation copyright © Terrance Dicks, 1987
Original script copyright © Robert Holmes, 1986
'Doctor Who' series copyright © British Broadcasting Corporation,
1986, 1987

The BBC producer of *Mysterious Planet* was John Nathan-Turner,
the director was Nicholas Mallett
The role of the Doctor was played by Colin Baker

Printed and bound in Great Britain by
Anchor Brendon Ltd, Tiptree, Essex

ISBN 0 426 20319 4

Contents

1

The Trial Begins

It was a graveyard in space.

A graveyard not of people but of ships. A junkyard, a scrap heap, a metallic cemetery, where the battered corpses of once-proud space-craft clustered together in a tangle of shattered hull plates and twisted girders.

The metallic desolation was clouded by drifting patches of cosmic dust, fitfully illuminated by the space lightning that crackled between the drifting wrecks.

But beyond the shattered space-ships there loomed something else. Something that was not derelict or destroyed but vast, powerful and massively whole, the integrity of its towering ramparts unbreached by the electrical storm that raged around them. It was a space station, one so huge as to seem almost a space city. Ovoid in shape with a colossal communications-tower sprouting from the centre, its entire surface was overlaid with spires and towers and battlements, with interlocking complexes of ornately designed buildings, workshops, laboratories, living quarters, energy-generators and space-docks, with batteries of space-cannon projecting from every available surface.

Massive, arrogant, invincible, the great complex hovered in space, dwarfing the shattered hulks that drifted around it, dominating its section of space like some enormous baroque cathedral. There was an eerie, almost mystical quality about it. It seemed to be brooding... waiting.

Suddenly the whole complex seemed to hum with titanic energies. A huge central hatchway irised open, emitting a great pillar of light, so intensely blue as to seem almost solid.

The pillar lanced onward and outwards, lancing into the furthest reaches of space. Somewhere in those infinite distances a shape appeared, trapped in the searching blue beam. A square blue shape with a flashing light on top and the words Police Box inscribed above its door.

Turning over and over in the powerful pull of the blue beam, swept downwards like a twig caught in a rushing waterfall, the TARDIS was drawn down and down until it reached the beam's very source, and vanished through the hatchway, disappearing into the heart of the space station.

The hatchway slid closed.

The TARDIS was trapped. And so, of course, was its occupant, that wandering Time Lord known usually as The Doctor....

The Doctor emerged from the TARDIS and stood looking around him. He felt puzzled, almost bemused, and he had a profound sensation that something was very, very wrong.

At this stage in his lives, in his sixth incarnation, the Doctor was a tall, strongly built man with a slight tendency towards overweight. Beneath the mop of curly hair, the face was round, full-lipped and sensual, with a hint of something catlike about the eyes. The forehead was broad and high and the jutting beak that was his nose seemed to pursue the Doctor through most of his incarnations. This Doctor was a solid, powerful figure, exuding confidence and energy, yet with something wilful and capricious about him. The extravagant side of his nature was reflected in his costume, which was colourful, to put it mildly.

The yellow trousers, vivid enough in themselves, were positively sober compared to a multi-coloured coat that might have made Joseph himself feel a pang of envy. Reds, yellows, greens, purples, and pinks, all in varying shades and hues, fought savagely for predominance. This quietly tasteful ensemble was finished off with a flowing cravat, a bright red affair with large white spots.

Clashing violently with the decor around him, the Doctor stood for a brief moment lost in thought. A profound sense of wrongness persisted. He ought not to be here. But then, where was here?

The Doctor looked around him. He was in a brief, broad corridor, one end empty and featureless, the other leading to a short flight of steps and an imposing door. One swift glance around him, and the Doctor knew effectively where he was.

This wasn't one of your blank, metallic, hi-tech spaceship, space-station, scientific installation type of corridors. The gleaming metallic walls had a rich golden hue, their expanse broken up by ribbed pillars and fussy grilles. The steps to the ornately decorated door were surrounded by a riot of castellated ornamentation.

Strange, thought the Doctor, how much you could tell about a culture from its taste in decoration. This particular culture was grandiose, pompous and obsessed with ritual. It was the culture the Doctor knew best in the entire cosmos – that of his fellow Time Lords.

He was in Time Lord territory.

It wasn't good news. The Doctor's relations with his Time Lord race had been varied to say the least. The variations had ranged from his being a hunted criminal and fugitive, an unwilling exile and press-ganged intergalactic agent to a tolerated eccentric, and on more than one occasion he had actually reached the eminence, unwanted though it was, of Lord High President of Gallifrey. Only the power of the Time Lords could have snatched him away from what he was doing. But then, what had be been doing?

With a shock of disquiet, the Doctor realized he couldn't quite remember. Still, no doubt it would come to him . . . in time. And as for where 'here' was, there was only one way to find out.

The Doctor mounted the little flight of steps and stood before the imposing set of doors.

He raised a hand to knock, changed his mind, shoved the heavy doors open with a powerful heave and strode confidently through.

He found himself in a huge vaulted chamber, furnished and decorated in the same elaborate style as the corridor without. The hall was dimly lit, and the Doctor could just make out the tall imposing figure that seemed to be seated opposite him.

The figure spoke in a deep, harshly resonant voice. 'At last, Doctor.'

'Am I late for something?' asked the Doctor politely.

The figure touched a control and light illuminated a small railed area which contained a large swivel-chair. 'Sit down.'

The Doctor sat and more lights came up, illuminating the figure opposite him, sitting in a railed area very similar to his own. The figure was that of a tall, gaunt-faced man wearing the long cloak, high-collared tunic and skull-cap like helmet of a Time Lord Court official.

This particular ensemble was all in black, and the Doctor struggled to remember its significance . One of those antiquated titles the High Council was so fond of – val something-or-other . . . Valeyard, that was it.

The tall, sinister figure opposite was the Valeyard. A Special Prosecutor working directly for the High Council, employed only in the most serious cases – especially those with political overtones.

Suddenly the Doctor realized he was in trouble.

'I was beginning to fear you had lost yourself, Doctor,' said the Valeyard sardonically.

The Doctor sat back in his chair. 'Even I would find it hard to lose myself in a corridor.' He swivelled round. 'Especially when propelled by the mental energy of so many distinguished Time Lords.'

To the Doctor's left were tiered rows of seats, like those in a lecture hall. The rear rows were packed with Time Lords, members of the High Council in their ornate high-collared robes. But the front row was empty, the Doctor noted – and so was the raised podium in front of it, with its single chair and simple table.

The elements were beginning to take shape, thought the Doctor. All that is needed now is . . .

The door at the far end of the room swung open, and a small imperious-looking woman entered, flanked by court officials and guards. She wore an elaborate head-dress and a white gown with a red sash of office. Not only the Valeyard but the Court Inquisitor as well, thought

11

the Doctor. They were really out to get him this time.

The Court officials filled the front row of the seating, and the Inquisitor took her place on the podium, settling into her seat with a rustle of robes.

The Doctor decided that it was best to keep up a pose of injured innocence. Nor indeed was it entirely a pose. Although he had a pretty clear picture of what was happening, he still had no idea why.

'Would it be too much to ask what all this is about?'

The Inquisitor settled into her place, folding her hands on the table before her, glancing around the room with an air of brisk efficiency. 'The accused will remain silent until invited to speak.'

The Doctor sat bolt upright with indignation. 'The accused? Do you mean me?'

The Inquisitor gave him a withering look. 'I call upon the Valeyard to open the case.'

Sweeping the Courtroom with his sombre gaze, waiting until the attention of the serried ranks of Time Lords was fixed upon him, the Valeyard launched into his opening address, rolling the legal jargon around his tongue with all the relish of a gourmet savouring a perfect meal.

'By order of the High Council, this is an impartial enquiry into the behaviour of the accused person, who will be known for the purpose of these proceedings as the Doctor. He is charged that he, on diverse occasions has been guilty of conduct unbecoming a Time Lord.'

The Doctor leaped to his feet and bellowed. 'Not guilty.'

No one took the slightest notice, so he sat down again.

Unperturbed, the Valeyard continued, 'He is also charged with, on diverse occasions, transgressing the

First Law of Time.' The Valeyard inclined towards the Inquisitor. 'It is my unpleasant task, Madam Inquisitor, to prove to this Inquiry that the Doctor is an incorrigible meddler in the affairs of other people and planets.'

There was a moment's silence as the Court absorbed the charges.

Studying the monitor screen built into her table-top for a moment. The Inquisitor said matter-of-factly, 'I see that it is on record that the Doctor has already faced trial for offences of this nature.'

The Valeyard said eagerly, 'That is so, My Lady. I shall also contend that the High Council showed too great a leniency on that occasion.'

Five years of exile on planet Earth thought the Doctor indignantly. Five years hard labour as Unofficial Scientific Adviser to UNIT. Call that lenient!

Although he had decided to keep the thought to himself, an amusing idea was entering his mind. Perhaps he had another card to play after all.

'Very well, Doctor,' snapped the Inquisitor. 'You have heard the charges. Do you have anything to say before the enquiry proceeds?'

The Doctor rose. 'Only that this whole thing is a farce. I am Lord President of Gallifrey. You can't put me on trial.'

With a general nod of farewell, the Doctor marched towards the door.

The clear cold voice of the Inquisitor stopped him in his tracks. 'Doctor!'

The Doctor turned, waiting.

'Since you wilfully neglected the responsibility of that great office, you have been deposed.'

'Oh,' said the Doctor, cast down. 'Is that legal?'

'Perfectly.' The Inquisitor smiled coldly. 'But we won't hold it against you.'

The Doctor walked back to his place in the dock and sat down thoughtfully.

'Quite the contrary in fact,' the Inquisitor went on. 'To see that your interests are fully protected, I propose to appoint a Court Defender, chosen from those Time Lords here present, to defend you.'

The Doctor studied the rows of impassive Time Lord faces.

'Ah! Thank you but – no thank you,' he said at last. 'I have been through several such inquiries before. I think it will be easier if I speak for myself.'

'Very well. The Court notes that the Doctor refuses the services of a Court Defender. Valeyard, you may proceed.'

The Valeyard rose once more, his sombre black-clad figure overshadowing the entire court room.

'Madam Inquisitor, I am not proposing to waste the time of the Court by dwelling in detail upon the activities of the accused. Instead I intend to adumbrate two typical instances for separate epistopic interfaces of the spectrum. These examples of the criminal behaviour of the accused are fully recorded in the Matrix, the repository of all Time Lord knowledge.'

Ah yes, the Matrix, thought the Doctor. The all-encompassing telepathic group-mind to which every Time Lord was attuned, in which was deposited all the knowledge and experience of those Time Lords who had exhausted their reincarnation cycles and passed on. The most valuable repository of information in the cosmos, accessible of course only to the Time Lords ... The disadvantage, of course, from the Doctor's point of view at the moment lay in the fact that everything he said and did, indeed, everything he thought and felt was recorded in the Matrix, and available for recall.

The Valeyard said impressively, 'I propose to begin with the Doctor's involvement with the affairs of Ravolox, a planet within the Stellian galaxy . . .'

A giant visi-screen appeared on the wall behind the rows of Time Lords. Moving as one, like puppets, they swung their chairs round so that they were facing it, and the Doctor, the Valeyard and the Inquisitor all swivelled their chairs for a clearer view.

The screen showed first a mist-shrouded planet hanging in space. Could have been anywhere, thought the Doctor. Any one of a million planets in a million galaxies. Could even be Earth, come to that. The planet loomed larger and larger till it blotted out the screen, and the picture changed to show two figures walking in a wood of tall trees.

The Doctor leaned forward eagerly. He loved a good story, particularly one in which he himself was the hero. And since his memory of recent events seemed to be a little hazy, the story unfolding on the screen might well be as new to him as it would be to the Court.

Well, thought the Doctor. So it begins . . .

But where would it end?

2

Underground

Sharing a big, multi-coloured umbrella between them, the Doctor and his companion strolled in fine drizzling rain through a wood that was made up of tall, widely spaced trees.

The Doctor wore his usual colourful attire. His companion, an attractive, dark-haired young woman, wore silver-grey slacks with a wide leather belt, a gold-coloured silk blouse, and a yellow blazer with diagonal stripes. It was a striking enough outfit in its way, though besides the Doctor's clashing riot of colours it seemed almost subdued.

The wearer of the outfit was pretty subdued at the moment. Her name was Perpegillian Brown, Peri for short. At the moment Peri was the Doctor's only companion in his wanderings, and like many a companion before her she was beginning to wish she'd stayed at home. There was something eerie about this silent, misty wood.

Peri looked around her and shivered. 'I don't think I like Ravolox very much. It reminds me of a wet November back on Earth.'

The Doctor looked down and smiled, amused as always by Peri's outspoken directness. Presumably it came from her American ancestry. 'That's part of the reason we're here,' he said encouragingly.

'Huh?' Peri put a world of scepticism into the monosyllable.

'Ravolox has the same mass, angle of tilt and period of rotation as Earth.'

'So?'

'Well, I thought that was quite interesting,' said the Doctor defensively.

'It's quite unusual to find two planets so similar. In fact, it's quite a phenomenon.'

Peri was looking deeply unimpressed. 'Really? Pity it couldn't have been a dry one.'

'Ravolox,' continued the Doctor, 'also has the distinction of having been destroyed by a solar fireball.'

Peri glanced around. 'It doesn't look very destroyed.'

'According to the records of Gallifrey, it was devastated by a solar fireball some five centuries ago. I think someone exaggerated, don't you?'

Noticing that the faint pattering of rain on his umbrella had stopped, the Doctor took it down, shook the water off it and furled it carefully. 'Ah the exhilarating smell of a freshly laundered forest,' he declaimed, inhaling lustily. 'You can't beat it.'

'The twittering of tiny birds,' added Peri sourly. 'The rustle of small mammals as they forage for food in the undergrowth.'

'Exactly!'

'Then you have better hearing than me,' said Peri triumphantly. 'There aren't any birds. Listen!'

They listened. Nothing but the same eerie silence.

'I wondered when you'd notice,' said the Doctor infuriatingly.

'None of this makes any sense, Doctor. Any soil left

17

after the visitation of a fireball would be sterile.'

'Well done.'

'Don't you patronize me, Doctor,' said Peri furiously. 'You knew from the start this amount of growth wouldn't be possible.'

The Doctor smiled. 'I also knew that as a student of botany you'd soon realize the truth without any prompting from me.'

Peri gave him a suspicious look. 'Maybe. Is there any intelligent life here?'

The Doctor smiled. 'Apart from me, you mean? I don't know. Shall we find out?'

He led the way onwards.

Doing her best to conquer her uneasy sensation that they were being watched Peri followed.

There was a very simple explanation for Peri's feeling that they were being watched.

They were being watched.

Introducing Sabalom Glitz – and his faithful assistant Dibber. Two intergalactic entrepreneurs.

Interplanetary businessmen with a wide-ranging field of interest – basically consisting of any field of activity that offered a fast grotzi and a quick getaway.

Glitz was a burly thick-set fellow with a tendency towards fatness. His tightly curled hair and elaborate whiskers gave him the air of an amiable bull. He was wearing his field gear, breeches and boots, topped with a somewhat flashy multicoloured jerkin with an elaborate layered epaulette on the right shoulder.

Dibber, taller and brawnier with a hard face and coarse bristly black hair, wore much the same outfit, except that his black-and-white-striped jerkin was sleeveless, worn over an ornately patterned shirt in blue and silver plasti-silk.

Both men wore cross-belts festooned with pouches and their appearance presented an odd mixture of the gaudy and the grim. They looked like pirates – which is exactly what they were. Dibber the muscle and Glitz the brains.

Slung over their shoulders were the chief tools of their trade – heavy-duty laser rifles.

They were watching the Doctor and Peri moving through the trees from their vantage position high up on a wooded slope.

Dibber frowned, his face taking on the pained expression that meant he was thinking, or trying to ... In fact, action, not thought, was Dibber's strong point. He left the thinking to Glitz.

'Well,' he said heavily after a lot of brow-knotting. 'They're not from round here, Mr Glitz.'

Dibber was never afraid to state the obvious.

'I know that, Dibber,' snarled Glitz.

Thoughtfully he watched the two strangers moving along through the tall mist-shrouded trees.

Something glinted on the ground ahead, catching the Doctor's eye. He bent down and scooped it up with the point of his umbrella, catching it neatly in his other hand.

'Aha, look at this!'

Peri looked. In the Doctor's hand was a crudely made necklace of roughly carved wooden beads.

'We are certainly not on this planet alone,' said the Doctor thoughtfully. 'Let's reconnoitre, shall we?'

19

He led Peri further along the slope.

Dibber and Glitz were fitting the telescopic sights on to their laser-rifles, doing so with a practised efficiency that made their movements seem almost automatic.

'You know, Dibber,' said Glitz conversationally, 'I'm the product of a broken home.'

Dibber nodded. 'You have mentioned it once or twice, Mr Glitz.'

It had been mentioned quite a few more times than that, actually. Glitz liked to talk, especially about himself. Dibber didn't mind. Listening to Glitz rattle on was all part of the job, and besides, it saved him the bother of having to talk himself.

'Well,' Glitz went on chattily, 'it sort of unbalanced me. Made me selfish to the point where I cannot stand competition.'

'Know the feeling only too well, Mr Glitz.'

Glitz didn't particularly care for that. How could a thickie like Dibber share the reactions of such a richly complex character as Sabalom Glitz!

He gave Dibber an offended look. 'Ah, but whereas yours is a simple case of sociopathy, Dibber, my malaise is much more complex. A deep-rooted maladjustment, my psychiatrist said, brought on by an infantile inability to come to terms with the more pertinent and concrete aspects of life.'

Dibber tightened the bolt on his scope. 'Sounds more like an insult than a diagnosis, Mr Glitz.'

'You're right there, my lad. Oh, I had just attempted to kill him, mind you. I hate prison psychiatrists, don't you? I mean, they do nothing for you. I must have seen dozens of them and I still hate competition – especially when it's poaching on my territory!'

Glitz adjusted the focus on his scope, and the Doctor's head sprang to life, clear and close in the cross-hairs. 'Oh, I'm going to enjoy this ...'

The bank suddenly became steeper and the Doctor skidded forwards, dropping a few feet. Peri jumped down after him ...

... and both the Doctor and Peri dropped out of sight, hidden by the curve of the land.

'Too late,' groaned Glitz, as the Doctor disappeared from the view-field of his telescope. 'Oh I do hate it when people get lucky. It really offends my sensibilities.'

As always, Dibber was concerned with the practical. 'Do you want me to go after them?'

Glitz wasn't listening. 'How is it they know where to look? Tell me that, Dibber!'

Dibber scowled. 'I dunno. Maybe they bought a copy of the same map we did. Do you want me to go after them?'

'Why?' snarled Glitz. 'Do you wanna help them?'

Sarcasm was lost on Dibber. 'No, it's just that if they're after the same thing we are ...'

Glitz seemed to have undergone one of his sudden changes of mind. 'Don't worry, they'll soon be dead anyway.' He sighed. 'It's just that I wanted the personal pleasure of killing them myself.'

*

Quite unaware of their narrow escape from death, the Doctor and Peri were moving on through the silent misty wood, making their way down the unexpectedly steep slope.

They seemed to be climbing down the side of some kind of mound, covered with earth and overgrown with thick vegetation. Something told Peri it wasn't a natural structure.

Something dull and metallic caught her eye, a rectangular shape almost completely concealed by a particularly thick clump of bushes.

Peri paused, and began pulling the bushes aside. 'Doctor, look!'

The Doctor came to her aid, and between them they had soon uncovered a section of metal panelling.

The Doctor studied it. 'It's the remains of a building...'

Peri saw the gleam in his eye. 'Doctor, we are not going inside.'

'Well, of course not,' said the Doctor reasonably. 'We can't, we haven't found the entrance yet! This is exactly the place where some early life-forms might have survived. Come along!'

He set off, clearly determined to find the entrance of the concealed building.

Reluctantly Peri followed. 'I'm just not crazy about meeting any of these early life-forms...'

But the Doctor ignored her.

Dibber and Glitz meanwhile were patiently removing the sensitive 'scopes from their weapons and packing them away in protective pouches.

Dibber had been thinking things over. 'Now we know we've got competition, going to the village could be a valuable waste of time.'

Thinking didn't come easy to Dibber, and sometimes his words got tangled on the way out.

Glitz sighed. He hated it when Dibber showed signs of independent thought, and began to elucidate, speaking in the slow careful voice of someone trying to explain atomic physics to a very small child.

'That complex down there is still functional, Dibber. Which means that the L-3 robot is still operational.'

'I understand,' said Dibber aggrievedly. Glitz had briefed him on their mission about fifty times already.

'To render the robot non-operational,' continued Glitz with the same exaggerated clarity, 'we have to destroy the light convertor which powers the robot's energy system.'

'I know all that.'

'Then why are you arguing with me, Dibber? It's not my fault if a bunch of backward savages have turned a Maglem mark seven light convertor into a totem pole.'

Dibber gestured towards the direction in which the two strangers had disappeared. 'It's just that I think we should kill those two first.'

Glitz gave him an outraged glare. 'And risk meeting the robot, head-on at full power? Sometimes I think you don't have my full interests at heart, Dibber.'

When Dibber managed to reach a conclusion he was reluctant to let go of it. 'If the robot doesn't kill them before we destroy his energy supply – well, they could be up and away with the goods before we even get back from the village.'

Glitz had already assessed this risk and decided that it

was one that had to be taken. He had decided to stick to his original plan. The arrival of the two strangers was a minor hitch that could be smoothed out later.

'I know, that, Dibber! Now you understand why I hate competition. It spoils everything.'

'I still think we should kill them first,' said Dibber obstinately.

Glitz smiled with evil anticipation. 'We will, Dibber, we will. When the time is right...'

The Doctor had found his door.

It was set into a concrete wall that was almost entirely concealed by a riot of vegetation.

Having found the door, the Doctor was struggling determinedly to get it open. It wasn't locked or fastened but it seemed to be stuck in some way, probably jammed by the fallen rubble inside.

Peri looked on worriedly. 'I know it sounds crazy, but I've got the weirdest feeling that I've been here before.'

The Doctor popped out of the tangle of vegetation and looked thoughtfully at her. 'I often get that feeling. Of course, in my case I usually have been here before! In yours, it's not possible.'

He returned to his door.

Peri said, 'Possible or not, I want to get away from here.'

'Absolutely right,' said the Doctor's voice, muffled by the overhanging vegetation. 'We've got to find out what's going on here.'

Despairingly Peri realized that he hadn't been listening to a word she'd said.

The Doctor gave a final heave. 'Aha, that's done it!

Come along Peri.'

He disappeared through the dark opening of the doorway, and reluctantly Peri followed.

She found the Doctor standing in some kind of anteroom, choked with rubble and half-blocked with twisted metal girders. He was illuminating the wreckage with a pocket torch fished from one of his capacious pockets.

Peri felt a sting on her hand. 'I seem to have scratched myself, Doctor.'

The Doctor was shining his torch beam across the cluttered chamber. There was something that looked very like the head of a staircase on the far side.

'Mmm?' said the Doctor absently. 'Oh, you're young, you'll soon heal.'

Picking his way across the rubble, he began descending the stairway.

Peri hurried after him. 'Thanks for the sympathy!'

It was a long steep staircase with metal treads and a black rubberized handrail and even in the gloom Peri found it hauntingly familiar.

The staircase led to a long narrow chamber, like a section of tunnel with a rounded roof. The Doctor and Peri separated, exploring.

The Doctor looked around him in fascination. 'You know, I'm glad I decided to come here. I might stay for a year or two and write a thesis. Ancient life on Ravolox by Doctor—'

Peri interrupted him. 'Doctor look! There's something here I think you should see.'

The Doctor went over to join her – quite unaware of the grotesquely masked spear-carrying figure watching them from the top of a shattered wall...

3

Barbarian Queen

Dibber and Glitz were still trudging determinedly towards the area where they believed they would find the native village. They realized they must be on the right track when a handful of spear-carrying skin-clad figures appeared in the woods ahead, loping stealthily towards them.

They ducked behind the cover of a sturdy tree.

'Look at them,' said Glitz disgustedly. 'Primitive screeds!'

Glitz hated primitive worlds. Unfortunately the police were too well-organized on the civilized ones, and a man had to take his business opportunities where he found them.

'Are they from the village?' asked Dibber, showing his usual lightning grasp of the obvious.

'Must be,' said Glitz wearily.

Dibber raised his laser-rifle. 'Let's make it so there's a few less for us to deal with.'

Glitz pushed down the barrel. 'No, no, all we need is a *gesture* of strength.'

He took a smooth metal cylinder from one of his belt pouches and lobbed it towards the advancing natives.

It landed on the path a little way ahead of them and exploded with a shattering report, sending up a shower of earth and leaves. When the smoke cleared, there wasn't a primitive to be seen.

Glitz beamed. 'Amazing the effect of a loud bang on the primitive mind!'

Realizing that no-one was dead, or even injured, the primitives reappeared from the woods and began advancing cautiously towards the waiting pair.

Glitz raised his voice. 'Come here, you ignorant, maggot-ridden peasant!'

As the leading primitive approached, Glitz glanced uneasily at Dibber. 'You know, I always feel foolish saying this bit.' Fixing the native with his most intimidating glare, Glitz muttered, 'Take me to your leader!'

The Doctor and Peri crouched down in the gloomy, litter-filled tunnel, studying Peri's find by the light of the Doctor's torch. The find consisted of a sizeable metal plate, and it was obviously the remains of some kind of sign-board or notice. It consisted of two words in white lettering on a blue rectangle. The rectangle itself was set against a white background, and surrounded by a red circle.

The two words on the sign read 'Marble Arch'.

'Well,' said the Doctor thoughtfully. 'I suppose there is a billion to one chance there was a place called Marble Arch on Ravolox.'

Peri gave him a scornful look. 'And they wrote in English?'

'That's another billion to one chance,' admitted the Doctor. 'It does begin to seem a little unlikely, doesn't it?'

27

'Doctor, we're on Earth, aren't we?' said Peri desperately. 'I said it felt like Earth.'

The Doctor frowned. 'It's in the wrong part of space to be your planet. Besides, according to all the records, this is Ravolox.'

Peri tapped the sign. 'Then how do you explain this?'

'Well, I can't, not yet. Unless of course, they collected railway stations.'

'That's ridiculous!'

'But not impossible, Peri. Not as impossible as the only other explanation.'

'What's that?'

'That somehow or other your planet and its entire constellation managed to shift itself a couple of light-years across space. After which, for some reason, it became known as Ravolox.'

'What time are we in?'

The Doctor produced a pocket chronometer and studied it. 'A long time after your period. Two million years or more.'

'So what happened to London?'

'Wiped out – if this was London, that is.'

'Oh, Doctor, I know it is – I can feel it!'

'Now don't get emotional,' said the Doctor severely.

'Don't get emotional?' Peri was outraged. 'This cinder we're standing on is all that's left of my world, everything I knew!'

Peri was near to tears.

In the Courtroom, the Doctor leaped to his feet. 'Why do I have to sit here watching Peri get upset, while two unsavoury adventurers bully a bunch of natives?'

The Valeyard said coldly, 'The reason will shortly be made clear, Doctor.'

The Doctor looked around the Courtroom. 'As a matter of interest, where *is* Peri?'

'Where you left her, Doctor.'

'Where's that?'

There was a note of mockery in the Valeyard's voice. 'You don't remember? Obviously a side-effect of being taken out of time. The amnesia should soon pass.'

The Inquisitor was becoming impatient with all this byplay. 'Shall we continue?' she enquired coldly.

It was more of a command than a request.

The Doctor sighed. 'Can't we just have the edited highlights?'

Very properly ignoring this frivolity, the assembled Time Lords turned their attention back to the screen.

The Doctor put his arm round Peri's shoulder. 'I know how you feel.'

'Do you?'

'Of course I do, Peri. But you've been travelling with me long enough to know that none of this really matters. Your world is safe.'

'This is still my world,' said Peri despairingly. 'Whatever the period. And I care about it. And all you do is talk about it as though we're in a planetarium.'

The Doctor sighed. That was the trouble with humans, he thought, they just didn't have the temporal perspective. 'I'm sorry . . . but look at it this way. Planets come and go, stars perish, matter disperses, coalesces, forms into other patterns. Nothing can be eternal.'

Peri sighed. 'I know what you mean. But I still want to

get away from here.'

The Doctor rose and began roaming restlessly to and fro. 'I can't leave yet. There's a mystery here, questions to which I must have an answer...' He paused, staring intently at a section of wall. 'Look, Peri – come here!'

He was wrenching at a handle set into the wall. He heaved, and a door opened with a faint hiss of air. 'Hermetically sealed,' muttered the Doctor. He peered through. 'It seems to lead down to a lower level. Some of the original inhabitants might have survived down there. Are you coming?'

Peri shook her head. 'No, I've seen enough. I'll wait for you at the entrance.' Peri sighed nostalgically, remembering her own time. 'Where they used to sell candy bars and newspapers...'

'All right. I shan't be long. Don't go wandering off. And be careful.'

The Doctor waved farewell and disappeared through the doorway. Peri turned away heading for the steps. Her foot turned on a fragment of rubble and she gave a little scream.

The Doctor popped out again. 'I said be careful!' Satisfying himself that Peri was all right he disappeared through the doorway again.

'Careful of what?' muttered Peri mutinously. 'The spooks and ghosts you're always telling me don't exist?' She looked round the surrounding gloom and shivered a little. 'You could have left me the umbrella,' she called.

There was no reply.

'Oh, please yourself,' said Peri. 'I don't mind getting wet!'

She turned back towards the stairs – and suddenly a grotesquely masked figure loomed up at her out of the darkness ... Then another ...

Primitive warriors, masked and carrying spears.

With terrifying speed they closed in on her.

Peri screamed.

The village could have been duplicated on many planets and in many times.

It was an archetypal primitive settlement. A low stone wall surrounding a variety of stonewalled thatched huts of assorted shapes and sizes. A larger building in the centre, primitive palace of some headman or chief.

A busy place, full of the activities needed for survival.

At a primitive forge a blacksmith was hammering a fragment of metal into a spearhead. A fur-clad woman boiled some kind of stew in a huge communal pot. Bands of children ran amongst the huts playing in the well-trampled mud.

Suddenly the peaceful scene was interrupted. A warrior in full battle-gear came running purposefully through the village. His war helmet with its built-in face-mask, intended both as a protection for its wearer and a means of terrifying his enemies, together with the long spear he carried, made him a grotesque and frightening figure.

Watched by the villagers, he disappeared inside the royal hut, which was distinguished not only by its size but by the gleaming metal pylon erected close by.

The silver tower caught the eye of Sabalom Glitz, as the little band of warriors, part escort, part captors, marched him and his companion into the village.

He nudged Dibber with his elbow. 'The light convertor.'

'Let me blast it, Mr Glitz,' whispered Dibber. 'Then we can get away from here.'

Glitz looked at the ferociously masked warriors surrounding them.

'Oh, you'd look good with a back full of spears, Dibber. Use your head.'

By now they were approaching the biggest hut – and a little group of natives was emerging to confront them. It consisted of impressive looking warriors and elders, and it was led by a formidable-looking woman.

Middle-aged and thick-set as she was now, it was clear that she must once have been very beautiful. She wore a long woven skirt, a white blouse and a woollen jerkin. Her many necklaces and her silver wrist-cuffs showed that she was a woman of wealth and position. The sickle-shaped crown with is central jewel, jammed firmly onto a head of blazing red hair, indicated that she was a queen. In her face, still strikingly handsome, there was the confident authority that comes with long-held power. Surrounded by the robed councillors, she stared impassively at the two newcomers.

Glitz nudged Dibber. 'We've got company – right royal company by the looks of things.'

Dibber looked at the stern set features and whispered, 'You'll never charm *her*, Mr Glitz.'

'I have an uncanny knack with ageing females, Dibber,' said Glitz confidently. 'One look into my eyes and they start to melt...'

Spreading his arms wide, smirking obsequiously, Glitz bowed low.

Dibber looked on dubiously. She didn't look the melting type to him...

After descending seemingly endless flights of stairs, the Doctor found himself in a different environment altogether. He was in a long, brightly lit corridor, with walls that curved upwards to form an arched roof. The white walls were ribbed, with a sort of venetian-blind effect, and they seemed to be luminescent in themselves, providing the source of the light.

The Doctor came to a junction and turned right into an even wider corridor. On his left there were three alcoves, each with a little flight of steps before it. The alcoves were flanked with long-necked glass vials set upon pedestals. Above each vial a long glass tube descended from the ceiling. Water dripped steadily from the tubes into the receptacles beneath.

Some kind of water-distillation set-up, decided the Doctor. Water would be at a premium so far below the surface.

He paused, looking uneasily around him. In quite extensive wanderings he hadn't seen a living soul, nor heard any sound other than the ever-present faint hum of machinery. It was a very different atmosphere from the eerily silent woods, or the gloomy rubble-strewn tunnels, but there was something odd and sinister about it all the same.

Perhaps only the machines had survived, thought the Doctor, maintaining this sterile environment for a race long dead and gone. But then, he thought, machines had no need of water.

He picked up the nearest vial and sniffed curiously at it. Yes, it was water all right. Pure distilled water.

As if to confirm this conclusion, an automated voice blared out. 'WATER THIEVES! WATER THIEVES! PROTECT YOUR WATER!'

Oval doors at the rear of the alcoves slid open and yellow-clad blank-faced figures poured out brandishing clubs.

The Doctor, as always, did his best to be friendly. 'Ah, how do you do, gentlemen. Perhaps you could direct me to the station master's office? I'm sure we can sort this out amicably . . .'

But the Doctor's friendly overtures were quite useless. Brandishing their clubs, the yellow-clad figures rushed upon him, and the Doctor went down beneath a hail of blows.

4

The Stoning

The immortal studied a console that was ablaze with flashing lights. The reading was clear. A life-form was present where no extra life form had the right to be.

The Immortal touched a control.

A monitor screen lit up above the console and a sombre-looking middle-aged man, black-clad and wearing a shiny black skull-cap, appeared on the screen, 'Yes, Immortal?'

The Immortal's voice boomed out. 'Marb Station shows one work unit over strength. Remove it.'

'Immediately, Immortal.'

The screen went dark and the Immortal turned away.

His massive metal body, with its terrifyingly blank curve of metal in place of a head, moved silently across the control room.

In a nearby sub-control room, the black clad man stood thinking for a moment. His name was Merdeen, and he was one of the most senior servants of Drathro the Immortal.

He moved across to where a red-overalled figure in a yellow harness and communications helmet sat at a console.

'Call the watch,' ordered Merdeen. 'Marb is a work unit over.'

The guard, whose name was Grell, stared unbelievingly at him. 'How?'

'I do not know. But the Immortal is never wrong.'

Grell nodded. 'I will summon the watch.'

His hands moved over the console.

Dibber was right. The queen – her name they had discovered was Katryca – didn't melt easily.

In fact, for all Glitz's smarmy charm, she was showing no signs of melting at all.

She had listened to Glitz's tale impassively. 'So, you are outlanders?'

'From a far-off star, your majesty,' said Glitz impressively.

If he was expecting an awed reaction he was in for a shock.

'You have a space-ship?' said Katryca matter-of-factly.

Glitz was taken aback. 'You have heard of such things?'

'It is recorded in our folk memory. Before the fire, our ancestors travelled among the stars.'

'Is that a fact?'

'It is also recorded,' continued Katryca coldly, 'that such star travel angered the gods, who punished us by sending the great fire which destroyed our planet.'

'No, dear lady,' protested Glitz. 'It was all much more secular than that.' He gestured towards the gleaming metal obelisk. 'That attracted the fireball.'

There was a shocked murmur from the crowd.

'That is our great totem to the earth-god Haldron,' said Katryca proudly.

'No madam,' said Glitz confidently. 'That is a malfunctioning navigational space beacon. It attracted the fireball five hundred years ago, and I am here to tell you that it is still malfunctioning today.'

'How do you know this?' demanded Katryca.

'It is my job to know. What's more, if you don't have it dismantled, the fireball will return.'

Katryca studied him thoughtfully. 'What is your name?'

'Sabalom Glitz, Your Majesty.'

'I am an old woman, Sabalom Glitz. You are not the first to visit my village from another world.'

'Is that a fact, dear lady?'

'Each and every one of them has wanted to dismantle the great totem.'

Small wonder, considering what it was worth, thought Glitz. But all he said was, 'In that case, you can surely understand the urgency—'

Katryca continued, 'yet each and every one of them had a different reason.'

'Let me assure you madam,' said Glitz smoothly, 'that my credentials are both bona fide and completely in order.'

He reached for his hand-blaster as he spoke, but before he could raise it, one of the warriors at his side wrenched it from his hand while another presented a spear at his throat.

Not without some difficulty, two more natives wrested the laser rifle away from Dibber.

Proudly, one of the warriors handed Katryca Glitz's hand-blaster.

'Ah, yes, the guns,' she said dryly. 'All the other outlanders had very similar credentials.'

'That totem is a navigational hazard,' spluttered Glitz indignantly. 'It must be dismantled.'

Katryca said, 'You must think me a fool. You have come here for no other reason but to steal the totem of our great god.'

'And what would I want with the symbol of some earth-grubbing deity?'

Katryca smiled. 'I do not know. But before you die, I shall certainly find out.'

Her warriors dragged them away.

Katryca hefted Glitz's blaster in her hand. 'Now Immortal,' she whispered, 'I am ready for you!'

The Doctor recovered consciousness to discover that he was bruised all over and lashed to a supporting pillar.

A very tall white-faced youth was staring super-ciliously down at him. Like the rest of the Doctor's attackers, he wore yellow coveralls and a sort of white linen helmet, shaped like a balaclava.

No wonder they all looked so eerily alike, thought the Doctor.

The tall youth said, 'Where are you from, old one?'

'Old one?' The Doctor glared indignantly at him.

'What station did you disgrace with your miserable presence, water thief?'

'Look, I may look old to you, whiskerless youth, but I'll have you know I'm in the prime of life. I'm not a day over nine hundred years old. Now, untie me at once.'

'You will be untied as soon as we are ready for the stoning.'

The Doctor noticed that quite a little crowd was gathering. They all seemed to be carrying baskets, the Doctor realized. And the baskets all seemed to be filled with rocks.

The Doctor turned back to his interrogator, who seemed to be in charge. 'Just who are you?'

'My name is Balazar. I am the reader of the books.'

'What books are those?'

'Ancient books from the world before the Fire. They contain much wisdom for those who can interpret their meaning. Here in Marb Station we have three.'

'Three? That's splendid! What are they called?'

'They are called the Books of Knowledge.'

The Doctor sighed. 'Each book must have its own name, Balazar. It's usually written on the front.

Importantly Balazar cleared his throat. 'One of our books is called *Moby Dick*, by Herman Melville. It tells of a great white water god, and has many mystical passages.'

'Yes, I've read it,' said the Doctor intrigued. 'What about the others?'

'How can you have read it?' demanded Balazar.' The sacred books belong to Marb – old one!'

'Will you stop calling me old one? I am known as the Doctor. What other books do you read?'

'*The Water Babies* by Charles Kingsley. This tells of life long before the Fire.'

'Sounds a rum sort of library to me. What's your third book?' Balazar lowered his voice. 'It is the most mysterious of all. It is called. "UK Habitats of the Canadian Goose". It is by HM Stationery Office.'

'What do you call this place?' asked the Doctor suddenly.

'Marb Station.'

'No, I mean the whole world, everything?'

Balazar gave him a puzzled look. 'It is called UK Habitat.'

Dibber stared moodily out of the barred window of the hut in which he and Glitz had been confined and saw a dishevelled, struggling figure being dragged through the village by two masked warriors.

'They've got that woman we saw earlier.'

Glitz wasn't interested. He was still brooding over his capture.

'I don't understand it, Dibber. They're savages.'

'Well, don't let it get you down, Mr Glitz.'

'What went wrong? That old hag took our guns away, just like that. How can *we* be *their* prisoners?'

Dibber shrugged philosophically. 'Told you it was risky, coming here.'

'Now you know what I mean about competition,' said Glitz bitterly. 'It gets you nowhere.'

'Told you we should have blasted them, Mr Glitz.'

'All right, Dibber, you've made your point!' snarled Glitz.

Dibber relapsed into an offended silence.

Balazar untied the Doctor and led him solicitiously to the centre of the open area, well away from the water vials. 'I think it best that you stand here.'

The Doctor looked round. 'Why?'

'In case some stray stone breaks the water vessels,' said Balazar reprovingly. 'People get very excited at these stonings.'

'I'm not excited,' said the Doctor.

Picking up his umbrella he turned to face the stoning squad.

Balazar stepped to one side. 'Ready?'

An excited murmur went up from the crowd. A good stoning was almost the only bit of entertainment they ever got.

'Steady ... go!' shouted Balazar.

As the first stones were hurled, the Doctor snapped open his big umbrella, using it as a shield. 'Roll up, roll up!' he taunted.

With a roar of disappointment, the stoners redoubled their efforts. For a time the Doctor was able to fend off the hail of missiles but suddenly a stray rock got under his guard, taking him in the temple.

The Doctor staggered back and fell...

In the Courtroom the screen went blank.

'Why stop it at the best bit?' protested the Doctor. 'I was rather enjoying that.'

'I'm sure you were, Doctor,' said the Valeyard.

'Clever, eh, that trick with the umbrella?'

'Most ingenious, Doctor.'

'Well, I always like to do the unexpected, take people by surprise.'

'See how he takes pride in his interference,' thundered the Valeyard. 'Hear how he boasts! This is not the behaviour of a responsible Time Lord.'

'We are aware of that, Valeyard,' said the Inquisitor coldly. 'What point are you trying to make?'

The Valeyard sprang to his feet. 'These proceedings

41

began as a mere Inquiry into the Doctor's activities. I now suggest that they become a Trial. And if he is found guilty I strongly recommend the termination of his life!'

5

The Reprieve

The Doctor sat back in his chair, and looked thoughtfully at the Valeyard. 'So you want me dead, eh?'

There is something very wrong here, thought the
Doctor. *Something very odd about this trial, or enquiry, or
whatever it is.* Time Lord justice could be politically
influenced, even corrupt at time, but this was something
quite extraordinary.

As if to confirm the Doctor's suspicions the Inquisitor
said, 'What the Valeyard wants and what the Court
decides are two entirely different things, Doctor.'

The Valeyard bowed, his sudden fit of anger choked
off.

The Doctor bowed too. 'Thank you, My Lady.'

'Proceed, Valeyard,' said the Inquisitor frostily.

The Valeyard bowed again, and the screen lit up.

Once again the Doctor saw himself felled by a rock
thrown at close range ...

There was a roar of triumph from the crowd as the
Doctor fell, and his attackers gathered round to finish
him off.

Suddenly an alarm siren cut through the excited
shouts.

Balazar held up his hands. 'The train guards!'

From out of the nearby tunnel an extraordinary vehicle glided into the open area. It was an electric truck with a uniformed driver at the controls and half a dozen guards sitting back to back in two rows of three on a trailer. Behind the driver sat the Chief Guard called Grell, the black-clad Merdeen beside him.

The little train glided to a halt, the guards jumped down and the yellow-clad work-units fell respectfully silent.

The dreaded train guards patrolled the tunnels day and night, alert for enemies from above ground or offences against the laws of the Immortal.

'This station is a work-unit over strength,' announced Merdeen. 'There must be a cull.'

Balazar stepped forward, pointing to the body of the Doctor. 'It is being dealt with,' he said proudly.

Merdeen studied the body curiously. 'See that he is dead, Grell.'

He turned to Balazar. 'Where is he from?'

'I do not know. He told many lies. He even said he had read our sacred books.'

Grell was kneeling by the Doctors body. 'He still breathes.'

'Then kill him,' said Merdeen.

Grell drew his blaster and put the muzzle to the Doctor's head.

In the main control room, Drathro the Immortal was studying the scene on his monitor.

'Stop!' he boomed.

Merdeen and Merdeen alone, heard the voice from the transceiver implanted in his helmet. 'Wait!' he ordered. 'The Immortal speaks.'

Grell lowered his blaster.

After a moment Merdeen said, 'The Immortal wishes to question the stranger. How near death is he?'

Grell put a hand to the pulse in the Doctor's neck. 'He is merely stunned.'

Merdeen turned to two of the guards. 'Pick him up.'

The guards hauled the Doctor to his feet.

Merdeen turned to Grell. 'Resume patrol.'

'Why not transport the stranger on the train?'

'Resume patrol.'

Grell glared angrily at him for a moment, but Merdeen's authority came direct from the Immortal.

Summoning the remainder of his guards he took his seat on the little train, which slid silently away.

Merdeen beckoned Balazar. 'You – come with me.'

Balazar recoiled. 'Me, sir?'

'You have spoken with the stranger. If he dies, the Immortal may wish to question you.'

Balazar shuddered, but followed Merdeen obediently away.

Peri was dragged through the village, hauled into the great hut and thrown down before an ornately carved throne.

From it a barbarically dressed middle-aged woman was staring impassively down at her.

'Hi,' said Peri weakly.

'Welcome, girl,' said Queen Katryca. 'Rise!'

Peri got to her feet, looking around her. She was in a

gloomy chamber, decorated with hideous-looking masks.

Before the throne was a huge round altar, on top of which burned some kind of sacred flame.

Masked spear-carrying warriors and ornately robed Councillors formed a guard of honour about the barbaric throne.

Katryca studied her captive for a moment.

'You are not from the place of the underground. Where do you come from?'

'It's difficult to explain.'

'My name is Katryca. I am the leader of the Free people. Do you have a name, girl?'

'Perpegillian Brown – but my friends call me Peri.'

Katryca studied her approvingly. 'Peri... Not many girls come to join the Free, Peri. I shall provide some excellent husbands for you.'

'Husbands,' asked Peri feebly. 'In the plural?'

'Such women as we have must be shared,' said Katryca impassively. 'Think about it. Put her with the other prisoners. Keep her guarded.'

A guard took Peri by the arm, but she pulled away. 'All right, all right, I can walk!'

The guards led her away.

The dazed Doctor was being half-dragged, half-walked, along the endless corridors by the guards.

Behind them Balazar and Merdeen strode side by side.

Balazar was recovering a little from his fear, and his ever-present curiosity was surfacing once more.

'Tell me, Merdeen, you serve the Immortal. Is he as men say?'

Merdeen gave him an ironical smile. 'What do men say?'

'That he is taller than two men, with arms of steel.'

'The Immortal is never seen. He stays in his Castle.'

'Then how does he give you his commands?'

'He talks to me through the air, and he watches me with . . . boxes, such as this.'

Merdeen pointed one of the omnipresent slave cameras mounted on the wall.

'I think that is called a camera, Merdeen,' said Balazar importantly. 'The men of ancient times used such things to make pictures of the sacred Canadian Goose.'

Merdeen looked curiously at him. 'How do you know this?'

'It is my task to study the ancient texts,' said Balazar proudly.

The Doctor had more or less recovered consciousness by now. He had a bad headache and he was in a filthy temper.

'As you continually boast,' he snarled, looking over his shoulder. 'That's the trouble with pallid little swots like you, Balazar. You can't even organize an efficient stoning!'

'It was only half over,' said Balazar defensively. 'If Merdeen and his Train Guards had not saved you . . .'

The Doctor stopped, bringing the little procession to a halt. He struggled to free himself, and Merdeen signalled to the guards to release him.

The Doctor said, 'I am grateful to you, Merdeen.'

'It was on the orders of the Immortal.'

'Well, please convey my thanks to him.' The Doctor noticed a flask at Merdeen's belt. 'I say, is that water? Could I have some?'

'It is my ration for the next two days.'

A voice boomed in Merdeen's ear. 'Give it to him.'

'Of course,' said Merdeen instantly. He reached for the flask, but the Doctor waved it away. It was a very small flask, he thought.

'I'm sorry, I'd forgotten how important that stuff is down here.'

Ever-curious, the Doctor peered up into the camera. 'A mono-optic system... interesting. Is the Immortal on the other end of that?'

The Doctor's inquisitive face filled the monitor screen in Drathro's control room.

The robot switched off the screen.

Incongruous beside Drathro's towering metal form, two small fair-haired youths stood ranked beside him. They wore white coveralls with yellow shirts and scarves and both had identical expressions of almost palpable smugness. After all, were they not the chosen ones, the elite, superior to all in the undergrounds, servants to the Immortal?

They had a tendency to get above themselves.

One was called Tandrell, the other Humker: apart from that they were pretty much identical.

Tandrell turned away from the monitor screen with relief. He hadn't cared for he look of the Doctor at all. 'He's extremely ugly.'

'Hideous,' agreed Humker. 'In the extreme.'

'Physiognomy is irrelevant,' boomed Drathro.

'In so far as—' began Tandrell.

'Appearance has no function,' went on Humker.

'But function has an appearance,' Tandrell pointed

out.

'Which is irrelevant to the function,' concluded Humker triumphantly.

'Perfect!' said Tandrell.

Humker clapped his hands. 'I must write that down.'

'I shall make an equation of it,' said Tandrell.

'Cease your prattle!' roared Drathro.

The robot studied them through its sensors. They had been chosen to serve the Immortal because theirs were the highest intellects available. Unfortunately they took their roles and their importance far too seriously, and insisted on intellectualizing everything. They enjoyed nothing more than demonstrating their own cleverness. Sometimes Drathro wondered if there was something wrong with the selection procedures.

'Activate the service robot,' he ordered.

'Of course, sir,' said Humker.

'Immediately, sir,' said Tandrell.

They scuttled to the console.

Peri was thrust into a very much smaller hut, with straw on the floor and bars on the windows. Its other occupants were two gaudily dressed but villainous-looking men.

The smaller and gaudier said, 'We seem to have a pretty visitor. I'm beginning to feel better already.' He bowed. 'My name is Sabalom Glitz, my dear. This fellow with the vacuous expression and single-track mind is Dibber.'

Peri decided she wasn't exactly crazy about her new room-mates. She also decided it might be safer to be polite. 'I'm Peri.' She studied them for a moment.

'You're obviously not from round here.'

'Merely visiting, like your good self,' said Glitz airily. 'I hope my visit's going to be a very short one.'

She peered through the barred window at the towering metal obelisk.

'That doesn't look as if it's from round here either.'

'It's a light convertor,' explained Glitz.

'It funnels black light energy down to the L3 robot,' explained Dibber earnestly.

Glitz silenced him with a look. 'I'm sure our friend Peri isn't interested in our professional problems, Dibber.'

'Yeah, of course... you're right, Mr Glitz.'

Resuming his smarmiest smile, Glitz turned back to Peri. 'When we first saw you, you weren't alone.'

'Yeah, that's right, said Dibber. 'You were with some dilly in a long coat. But you dropped out of sight before we could—'

'Before we could leap out and make your acquaintance,' interrupted Glitz hurriedly.

'Yeah, that's it,' agreed Dibber.

'Er – where is your friend now?' asked Glitz casually.

'The Doctor? Oh, he's probably still down there somewhere – underground. For a Time Lord he's not very good at keeping time.' Dibber and Glitz exchanged glances.

'So your friend the Doctor is a Time Lord,' said Glitz thoughtfully.

'That's how he knew where to go.'

Peri looked puzzled. 'What do you mean?'

'They sent him, did they?' asked Dibber.

'Who?'

'The Time Lords, my dear,' said Glitz. 'As my friend

says, he must be acting on their behalf.'

Peri shook her head. 'The Doctor seems to have broken off from the Time Lords. I doubt is he's acting on anyone's behalf.'

Immediately Glitz looked relieved. 'A freelance, eh? Like myself...' He glanced at Dibber. 'Possibly we can reach an accommodation here my boy. Two rogues with but a single thought!'

The little procession was moving on its way. 'How long has the Immortal lived in his so-called Castle?' asked the Doctor.

Balazar said, 'Since the Fire.'

'Five hundred years?'

'I do not know, he was sent to save our lives many centuries ago.'

'And he never goes out and nobody goes in?'

'Only those young men who pass the Selection.'

'What selection?'

'To find the two cleverest youths. They go to the Castle.'

'Why?'

Balazar hesitated. 'It is said the Immortal eats them.'

51

6

Meeting the Immortal

The Doctor looked hard at Balazar for a moment, but it was clear that he was perfectly serious.

'Never believe what is said, Balazar,' said the Doctor softly. 'Only what you know.'

They continued on their way.

The Service Robot was square and massive, shaped unpleasantly like a tombstone. The central section was black with a bright disc set into the top, like a single blazing eye. Two segments, one on either side, were picked out in yellow, and there was a servo-camera mounted on the top.

Huge and menacing, the Service Robot glided along the corridors, watched nervously on the monitor screen by Humker and Tandrell.

'Why are we doing this?' demanded Humker.

Tandrell glanced over his shoulder at the metal shape towering over them. 'Because Sir ordered it,' he said piously.

'It may be needed,' boomed Drathro, and all discussion was at an end.

*

Dibber rattled moodily at the wooden bars on the window of their prison hut.

One was already broken off, and the rest looked as if they would go without too much effort.

Of course, there were still the armed guards surrounding the hut...

'These bars remind me of home,' growled Dibber. 'I reckon I could bite me way through them.'

Glitz was stretched out, his back against the wall. 'Relax, Dibber, I'll soon find some way of winning the confidence of these simple peasants.'

Peri was even more restless than Dibber. 'I'd like to get out of here. That Katryca said something about choosing some husbands for me.'

Glitz smiled. 'There you are Dibber! Obviously the good queen is a romantic at heart.'

'So am I,' said Peri. 'But not romantic enough to want more than *one* husband.'

'Where we come from, a woman can have as many as six,' said Dibber conversationally.

Peri smiled, remembering the marriage records of certain Hollywood film stars. 'It can happen on my planet too – only they usually have 'em one at a time!'

'I should like to stand in the role of paterfamilias for your absent father and give you away,' said Glitz sentimentally. 'Unfortunately I always cry at these moments of deep sentiment.'

Dibber had taken a liking to Peri. 'I think we should help her to get out, Mr Glitz.'

'No, no, dear boy. We may need these brutish primitives.'

'Need them for what?' asked Peri curiously.

Glitz produced a folded map from inside his tunic.

'This shows the layout of the tunnel system, all hermetically sealed. If we can persuade Katryca's people to drive a shaft down into the centre of the system we can fill the tunnels with gas.'

Peri was horrified. 'Kill them? The people Katryca called underground dwellers? That would be mass murder.'

Glitz looked pensive. 'I'm sure my conscience will prick a little.' He brightened. 'But where money is concerned, that doesn't usually last long.'

'You can't do it!' protested Peri.

'Oh, I think it'll be pretty simple,' said Glitz. 'Don't forget, Peri, this is a high-risk, high-profit venture. The people down there take the risk, and I take the profit!'

'That still leaves the L3 robot,' pointed out Dibber.

Glitz laughed. 'And what chance would the robot have without a labour force? Tell you what, Dibber this'd probably be quicker than trying to knock out its black light supply.'

The door of the hut was thrust open and Glitz hurriedly thrust the map away.

A tall, bearded man in a hooded smock appeared in the doorway. He had a distinctive snaggle-tooth in the centre of his mouth, and Peri recognized him as one of the Councillors who had been at the queen's side.

He was in fact, her chief adviser, known, not surprisingly, as Broken Tooth.

'Come with me,' he ordered.

He wasn't armed, but there were guards at his back. Dibber, Glitz and Peri followed him from the hut.

They were marched through the village and into the great hut, where Katryca sat chin in hand on her throne, her guards and councillors about her staring into the sacred flame that danced upon the altar.

Glitz bowed low and smiled. 'Dear lady, I knew that once you had time to consider—'

'Silence, fat one,' snarled Katryca. 'I have studied the sacred fires and there is anger in them. You have travelled from beyond the stars, your intention to steal our great totem. Only a sacrifice in the flames will propitiate the god.'

'All of us?' asked Dibber, practical as ever.

Katryca shook her head, jabbing a bony finger towards Glitz. 'No. Only you are the chosen one, Sabalom Glitz.'

Glitz was outraged. 'Me? Are you insane? I'm wanted in six different galaxies for crimes you couldn't even imagine. Do you think an old hag like you can bring me down?'

Katryca was unimpressed. 'The pyre is being built. You will be brought forth when your time is due.'

She waved them away.

The tunnel widened and ended in a massive set of double doors.

'You enter here, Doctor,' said Merdeen.

'Ah! No need to knock I take it?'

'Will I be needed?' asked Balazar nervously.

Merdeen listened to the voice inside his helmet for a moment. 'No.'

Balazar looked comically relieved and the Doctor grinned. 'Lucky old you!'

Merdeen said sternly. 'When you are in the Immortal's presence, Doctor, you will cast your eyes to the ground.'

'Will I?'

'It is forbidden to look upon him.'

'On pain of being turned into a pillar of salt, I imagine. That sort of thing?'

'You will not find it wise to mock the Immortal,' said Merdeen threateningly. 'Doubtless your body will be returned to me for disposal before the day is out.'

The Doctor put a friendly arm about his shoulders. 'Merdeen, why don't you just push off and guard some trains or something, hey?' Patting Merdeen on the back the Doctor thrust him gently away and strode up to the doors.

They were high and arched, patterned in some silvery metal. He thrust hard at them and they swung open without resistance. The Doctor marched through the doors and they swung closed behind him.

Merdeen and Balazar and the guards moved away. As they did so, a massive black and silver shape glided from an alcove and took up its station before the doors.

The Service Robot was on guard.

The Doctor found himself in a sort of metallic ante chamber, with another set of double doors on the far side.

One of the omnipresent cameras was mounted above the doors, and the Doctor strode up to it, presenting his left profile to the lens.

'This is my best side.'

Humker and Tandrell watched him on the monitor.

'The arrogance,' breathed Humker.

'Can't wait to see how he's been programmed,' said Tandrell.

The inner doors swung open and the Doctor appeared. Completely ignoring Merdeen's instructions, he stared in fascination at the towering form of the robot, scarcely noticing the two white-clad acolytes bobbing about in front of it.

'Welcome,' said Drathro. 'I have long been waiting for this day. Welcome at last!'

'You've been expecting me?'

'For centuries. I am Drathro, an L3 Robot.'

'Then I fear you are under a slight misapprehension, Drathro,' said the Doctor. 'I only decided to come here yesterday.'

'You are not from Andromeda? Then where are you from?'

'Gallifrey, originally. But I travel a lot.'

'I have heard of Gallifrey. An advanced civilization.'

'In some ways,' said the Doctor.

'I apologize for my error.'

'That's all right,' said the Doctor generously. 'Even immortals make the odd mistakes every few millenia.'

'I am not immortal.'

'Ah! Well, the locals seem to think you are.'

The robot gestured towards the two white-clad figures. 'These are my assistants, Tandrell and Humker. You will work with them.'

'Will I? Why?'

'Because I command it.'

'I see,' said the Doctor thoughtfully. 'And obviously you're a robot who's used to getting your own way.'

Humker and Tandrell crowded round the Doctor, prodding and poking at him. 'This is remarkable,' said

Humker.

'Most impressive,' agreed Tandrell.

'Even its texture has organic warmth,' said Humker amazed.

'Do stop prodding me, there's a good fellow,' said the Doctor.

Drathro boomed, 'The Doctor is not a robot. He is an organic from an advanced civilization.'

Tandrell was amazed. 'An organic?'

'We have not met an organic since we passed the Selection,' said Humker.

'Aha!' said the Doctor. 'I knew you two hadn't ended up for lunch.'

'Explain,' said Tandrell.

The Doctor waved him away. 'Never mind.' He looked up at Drathro. 'What is this work you want me to do?'

'Is this relevant testimony, Valeyard?' asked the Inquisitor testily. 'We seem to be straying from the point.'

'The testimony is circumstancially germane, My Lady,' insisted the Valeyard. 'It forms part of the prosecution's case that the Doctor introduces a disruptive and corrupting influence wherever he goes.'

'Sheer poppycock,' said the Doctor briskly.

The Valeyard's voice quivered with anger. 'If the Doctor had not visited Ravolox, the whole chain of events we are witnessing would never have been set in motion.'

'How can the boatyard make that claim?' shouted the Doctor. 'What might or might not have happened is purely speculative.'

'That is for me to decide, Doctor,' said the Inquisitor. Quite clearly, she was not amused. 'May I remind you that the charges you face are grave indeed?'

'I have only to look at the graveyard to see that, My lady,' said the Doctor, going rapidly from bad to worse.

'Your puerile attempts at flippancy are not appreciated in this Court, Doctor. Proceed Valeyard.'

The screen came to life once more.

With the help of Tandrell and Humker, the Doctor had removed the casing from an enormous control console and was now elbow-deep in the complex circuitry inside.

Drathro hovered impatiently over him. 'Have you found the fault yet?'

The Doctor looked up. 'Give me a chance, I've just started.'

'The black light system is indicating incipient failure,' boomed Drathro.

'I can see that,' snapped the Doctor. 'They don't last forever, you know.'

'I am trained only in installation and maintenance,' said the robot.

The Doctor was buried inside the console again. 'What? Oh, very useful too, that's where the money is.'

'I have trained these humans to study the problem, but they make no progress,' said Drathro almost plaintively.

'Well, black light is very tricky stuff, Drathro...'

'I have a learning capacity, but my process of ratiocination are strictly logical. Organics sometimes eliminate such steps.'

The Doctor went on working. 'It's called intuition,' he said absently.

'Your first task will be to restructure the system.'

'Now just a minute,' protested the Doctor. 'Black light just isn't my field.'

'Then you will make it so – or die!'

In the Courtroom the Doctor leaped to his feet. 'I protest!'

The Inquisitor said wearily, 'What now?'

'Yes, now!'

'I mean what are you protesting *about* Doctor?'

'I am charged with interference, yet it is obvious to a blind sneelsnope that I am working under duress.'

The Inquisitor considered. 'That does seem a valid point. What is the relevance of this presentation, Valeyard?'

'If the accused had not interrupted, My Lady, the point I wish to make would have become obvious.'

'Then I apologize for my outburst, My Lady,' said the Doctor handsomely.

'As Your Ladyship is aware, unlike the Valeyard I am unfamiliar with court procedure.'

For the first time the Inquisitor mellowed a little. 'The Court accepts your apology, Doctor,' she said graciously. 'Valeyard, you may proceed.'

The screen lit up once more. This time it showed the village of the Free people. They were building a pyre.

Peri, Dibber, and most particularly Glitz, watched unhappily as the eager hands of the villagers piled brushwood around the foot of a sinisterly charred wooden stake.

They laughed and chattered excitedly as they worked. For the villagers a public burning was the equivalent of a stoning to the underground dwellers – one of the few bits of entertainment in an otherwise dull existence.

'What a terrible waste,' said Dibber.

'You're telling me,' said Glitz, the intended victim, touched by his taciturn colleague's concern.

'No, I meant the wood,' explained Dibber. 'If I was handling this execution I'd go for a bullet in the back of the neck. Much more economical.'

'He has a point,' said Peri.

Glitz glared reproachfully at them. 'Of all the snivelling screeds to be stuck with in my moment of need I have to get you two!'

'Depressing innit,' said Dibber.

Their guards prodded them back towards the prison hut. There was still a lot of work to be done on the pyre.

The Doctor straightened up. 'Sorry, Drathro, there's not a lot I can do down here.'

'I order you to work.'

'You can play the slave-driver all you like, but the fault doesn't lie down here at all. There must be a malfunctioning collection aerial up there on the surface. I'll just pop up and take a look at it for you.'

The robot barred his way. 'You will remain here and proceed with your task.'

'I think you must have fluff in your audio circuit,' said the Doctor reprovingly. He looked round the equipment-crowded control room. 'What's all this stuff for, anyway?'

'It provides Drathro with his energy source,' said Humker.

'It was intended also to maintain the three sleepers till they could be returned to Andromeda,' said Tandrell.

'The three sleepers?'

The Doctor was beginning to piece the story together. Drathro had been installed by an expedition from Andromeda, designed perhaps to save some of the natives of the planet from the effects of the approaching fireball, by setting up an underground survival system. But something had gone terribly wrong.

'The sleepers are dead now,' said Drathro. 'The relief ships failed to arrive.'

Three Andromedan astronauts in suspended animation, thought the Doctor. Waiting for a back-up expedition that never came. But the fireball had been less devastating than had been feared, and life had gone on, on the surface and underground...

But that was all in the past, thought the Doctor. An equally terrible crisis now menaced them in the present.

'Now, listen,' said the Doctor urgently. 'If this black-light power failure is allowed to get any worse, we'll all be as dead as your three sleepers.'

Humker stared at him. 'Why?'

'Because there's going to be a most enormous explosion, that's why! An explosion in which everyone in your precious underground colony will be destroyed!'

7

Escape

'You must listen,' said the Doctor urgently. 'I can't impress upon you enough how urgent it is that I go outside and look at that convertor aerial.'

Drathro refused to listen. 'A transparent ruse to escape. Go on with your work.'

The Doctor looked at his two assistants. 'How do you stand him?' He paused. 'Tell me, why is water so all-important down here?'

'The condensation plants produce only enough for five hundred work-units,' said Humker.

'But it was raining buckets outside when I arrived.'

'Precipitation on the surface has returned to normal,' confirmed Drathro.

'Then why don't you let them all pop up and help themselves?'

'I was programmed to maintain an underground survival system.'

Typical robot behaviour, thought the Doctor. The system must be maintained though the need for it was long gone. 'Inflexible little fellow aren't you?' he muttered. 'Well, if you want me to carry on here, you'll have to help me. Come on, aren't you programmed to be user-friendly?'

He held out a lead, and the robot grasped it in a clamplike hand.

'At times like this one needs at least three hands,' said the Doctor chattily. 'You know, we bipeds are really a very inefficient design. You, Humbug, whatever your name is, hold that. And you, Handbag, you hold this one.'

When all three were holding leads, the Doctor said, 'that's it, yes. Splendid!'

He threw a power switch and electricity surged through the console – and through Humker, Tandrell and Drathro, who stood fixed, vibrating in the current.

The Doctor turned and ran, out of the control room, across the ante-room and out into the main corridor – where he found his way barred by the Service Robot.

'Look!' shouted the Doctor.

Pointing to the left, he hared off to the right.

The Service Robot hovered indecisively.

Drathro snatched himself free from the console, cut the power and strode into the corridor.

'Follow him,' he ordered. 'Use your tracer disc. He must be brought back – unharmed!'

The Service Robot glided away in pursuit of the Doctor.

The prisoners were nearly back to the hut when Glitz decided it was time to make a move.

He caught Dibber's eye. 'Ready?'

Dibber nodded.

'Run, Peri,' shouted Glitz.

Peri ran.

Instinctively the guards pursued her – which put Dibber and Glitz behind them. It was a bad mistake.

Peri had run only a few yards when she heard gasps and the thud of blows. She turned and saw the first guard tripped by Glitz and knocked cold with the butt of his own spear. In the same moment Dibber had clubbed the second guard to the ground with three savage blows from forearm, fist and knee.

'Well done, Dibber,' panted Glitz. He produced a metal cylinder from under his tunic. 'Here take this. Always keep something up your sleeve, eh Dibber?' He grinned. 'Now, my lad, I want you to conceal yourself in some muddy crevice while Peri and I lead off the hunt.'

'What hunt?' asked Peri. So far their escape seemed to have passed unnoticed.

Glitz pointed. In the distance a tall bearded figure was staring at them in horror.

It turned and began running towards the Queen's hut.

'There'll be a hunt soon,' predicted Glitz confidently. 'Now Dibber, as soon as you can get the chance, I want you to blow that convertor to bits.'

Dibber took the grenade. 'Right. Where do we meet up?'

'The entrance to the tunnel. Come on, Peri.'

They turned and ran from the village, heading for the woods.

Katryca was studying the sacred flame for omens when Broken Tooth dashed into the hut, shattering all the rules of etiquette.

'How dare you?' screamed Katryca.

Broken Tooth fell to his knees. 'Forgive me, Majesty. The prisoners have escaped!'

Katryca snatched up Dibber's laser rifle which was

propped against her throne.

As Broken Tooth got to his feet, she tossed him the weapon.

'Take this. Lead the young men in a hunting party. They must not escape.'

Catching the gun, Broken Tooth ran from the Royal hut, bellowing for his warriors.

As the Doctor hurtled down the tunnel, running for his life, Merdeen, travelling through the corridors with Balazar and the two guards, heard the familiar voice of the Immortal through his helmet-speaker. 'The Doctor has absconded. He must be found.'

'Yes Immortal.'

Merdeen raised his hand, bringing the little party to a halt. He stood listening to the Immortal's instructions, then motioned his party onwards.

In the control room, Humker rubbed tingling fingers. 'He should be killed.'

'Very slowly,' agreed Tandrell. 'He hurt me. I hate being hurt.'

'He hurt me more,' said Humker.

'That is a subjective judgment!'

'He must not be killed, bellowed Drathro. 'I need him!'

The Service Robot sped along the corridors, the tracer disc glowing brightly as it tried to pick up the fleeing Doctor.

*

Merdeen halted his party at a tunnel junction. He turned to the two guards. 'You, search Area Red. You, Area Green.' The two guards moved away.

Merdeen led Balazar to an nearby alcove.

Ever conscientious, Balazar said worriedly, 'Should we not be searching for the Doctor?'

'Quiet,' said Merdeen. He looked around, lowering his voice. 'You are a clever man, Balazar.'

'I am the Reader of the Books,' said Balazar proudly.

'People like you are needed on the surface. I can direct you there!'

'The surface? But nothing lives there! The Fire—'

'There is no Fire. There has been no Fire for hundreds of years. On the surface you will be beyond the Immortal's reach. Do you understand me?'

Balazar nodded doubtfully, grappling with this new thought.

Suddenly he realized that he wanted to see the surface very much indeed. Somehow Merdeen had sensed that he was ripe for rebellion.

'But what shall I do, Merdeen. How will I live?'

'You will find others out there,' said Merdeen proudly. 'Many of them I have saved from the Immortal.'

'If the Immortal discovered this, you will die,' said Balazar slowly. 'Why do you risk your life, Merdeen?'

'I am sick of the Cullings,' said Merdeen simply.

It was explanation enough. To keep the numbers constant at the sacred five hundred, periodic Cullings took place, in which men, women, even children, were taken away and brutally killed. Balazar, like every underground dweller had lost friends and family to the Cullings. His own turn would come one day . . . He had always accepted them as an inevitable fact of life – until now.

'I have to be very careful,' Merdeen went on. 'I think Grel suspects me already.'

'What will you do now? asked Balazar.

'Find the Doctor and send him to you,' said Merdeen. 'Come!'

As they moved away, a helmetted figure appeared from the shadows of a nearby alcove.

It was Grel.

Peri and Glitz were running through the woods, like hunted animals. Not far behind came the hunters from the village, led by Broken Nose, laser-rifle in hand. Glitz was panting hard, and beginning to fall behind.

Dibber waited until the attention of the village was fixed on the escapers and the hunt, then emerged cautiously from behind an empty hut.

Setting the timing on the grenade, Dibber placed it carefully at the base of the gleaming obelisk, then dashed for the shelter of a nearby hollow.

As he hurtled into the dip, stretching face-down in the muddy ground, he heard the crack of the explosion behind him, and turned in time to see the obelisk topple. With a grin of satisfaction at a job well done, Dibber scrambled to his feet and set off for the woods.

Seconds later, the villagers began boiling from their huts like angry bees . . .

*

Arcs of electricity crackled like lightning around the control room, and even Drathro staggered about disorientated.

'What is happening?' he roared.

Humker and Tandrell wrestled with the console to no avail.

Broken Tooth paused for a moment to check the sign on the ground before him. He rose. 'This way!'

The hunters sped on.

Haring along a corridor the Doctor ran smack into Balazar and Merdeen.

'Whoops!' he shouted and spun round to flee.

'Wait, Doctor,' called Merdeen. 'We mean you no harm.'

The Doctor turned to face them. 'You did last time we met.'

'Things have changed,' said Balazar earnestly.

'Then let me pass,' said the Doctor. 'I have to get out of here.'

'Then take Balazar with you, pleaded Merdeen.

Yes all right,' said the Doctor, in too much of a nurry to ask for explanations.

'What will you do, Merdeen?' asked Balazar.

'I'd be careful if I were you,' said the Doctor. 'There's a robot following me who isn't in a very friendly mood.'

'Will you return to help us, Doctor?' asked Merdeen. 'Help us to crush the Immortal's power?'

'Perhaps, if I can,' said the Doctor hurriedly. 'But there's something very important I must do first. Come along, Balazar!'

The Doctor and Balazar ran, heading for the route to the surface. Merdeen looked after them for a moment, then turned and went the other way.

The Valeyard halted the proceedings to address the Court once more.

'This, as you see, is another example of the Doctor's interference. You note that he was in a position to free himself from the situation, yet chose not to do so.'

The Doctor was on his feet. 'I was trying to *help*! Surely even a blockhead like you can see that.'

'The Inquisitor intervened. 'I think we should reserve judgment till the end of the sentence.'

The Doctor glared at the Valeyard. 'I agree,' he snapped. Then he gave the Inquisitor his most charming smile '—My Lady.'

The Doctor sat down... and saw himself emerging from the underground tunnels, Balazar close behind him.

Balazar looked at the forest in sheer amazement. 'It's beautiful...'

The Doctor however was looking around for Peri, irrationally annoyed to find she wasn't there. 'Oh, I knew she wouldn't still be here – that girl just can't obey an order.'

Suddenly a familiar figure came pelting through the trees towards them. A voice called, 'Doctor!'

It was Peri, Glitz puffing behind her.

The Doctor waved. 'Peri!'

A third figure appeared.

It was Dibber arriving from the village.

The hunting party spotted him, and increased their pace. Broken Tooth paused to take aim with the laser-rifle. Unfortunately no-one had shown him how to use it. He gave up and resumed the chase.

Peri dashed up to the Doctor, and he waved her inside. 'In you go, back inside. You too, Balazar.'

Peri and Glitz hurried back inside, and Balazar followed. Dibber dashed up, and shot inside after the others, and the Doctor followed last.

With a howl of rage, the hunting party converged on the tunnel entrance.

Glitz collapsed gasping just inside the entrance. 'I always knew exercise was bad for you.'

The Doctor bustled past him. 'I shouldn't lie there if I were you, not unless you want a spear in your back!'

'What!' Hurriedly Glitz scrambled to his feet. He caught Dibber's arm. 'Did you do the job, my boy?'

'Course,' said Dibber, and Glitz noded contented.

'Come on,' called the Doctor. 'We've got to get out of here!'

He led them down the long steep flight of steps and into the lower tunnel – only to find himself facing the Service Robot. He turned to retreat – and saw Broken Tooth and his warriors blocking the head of the stairs.

'Now what?' shrieked Peri.

The Doctor looked ahead to the Service Robot and behind to the hunters. Broken Tooth at their head was raising the laser rifle.

For once even the Doctor didn't have an answer. 'I

don't know,' he said. 'I really think this could be the end!'

8

Captives of Queen Katryca

Broken Tooth fiddled wildly with the mechanism of the laser-rifle, and a wild blast smashed rubble from the tunnel ceiling.

Suddenly Balazar shouted. 'I know him – it's Broken Tooth!'

'Then why doesn't he fire at you?' yelled Glitz.

'Broken Tooth, it's me! ' shouted Balazar.

Confused, Broken Tooth stared wildly at him.

'Fire at the Robot!' shouted the Doctor.

'Shoot the Immortal One,' called Balazar.

Slowly Broken Tooth raised the rifle. 'Down everyone!' yelled the Doctor.

'Squeeze the trigger gently, don't pull it,' called Dibber.

The Service Robot glided forwards – and Broken Tooth fired. This time he got it right.

The blast caught the Service Robot full on its casing and it ground to a halt, de-activated. As everyone clambered to their feet the Service Robot stayed silent and still.

In the control room, Drathro stared at a blank monitor screen.

'What is happening? Reactivate!'

Humker and Tandrell worked frantically at the Robot's controls.

'We're trying, Immortal,' called Humker.

'It doesn't respond,' said Tandrell.

'You must make it work,' ordered Drathro. I must have the Doctor back here. My black-light system is failing!'

The native hunters gathered curiously around the de-activated robot, while the Doctor and Peri conferred with Broken Tooth and Balazar.

'I can't believe you're alive, Broken Tooth,' Balazar was saying. 'They said you'd been culled.'

'I owe my life to Merdeen,' said Broken Tooth simply.

'I too,' said Balazar excitedly.

'I hate to break up this happy reunion,' said the Doctor. 'But I have to find the aerial to Drathro's black-light convertor.'

Dibber stepped forward. 'No need to hurry – it's gone.'

'Gone where?'

'I blew it up,' said Dibber proudly.

The Doctor was horrified. 'What?'

'It'll put the L3 robot out of action,' Glitz pointed out.

'It'll start an explosive chain reaction more likely,' said the Doctor. 'Drathro's black light system is highly unstable. Blowing it up is about the worst thing you could have done!' he turned to go. 'I must go and shut the system down right away.'

Suddenly Broken Tooth raised the laser-rifle, and taking their cue from him, his warriors raised their spears.

'You will all return to our village,' announced Broken Tooth. He pointed at Glitz. 'Our Queen has unfinished business with this person.'

'No!' protested the Doctor.

Broken Tooth swung the rifle to cover him. 'You will all come with us – and you will all come quietly.'

Glitz jabbed Dibber in the ribs. 'And you had to show him how to use the gun!'

This time it was the Inquisitor herself who halted the proceedings.

'Valeyard, are these unpleasant scenes of primitive violence necessary to your case? I find them distressing.'

'I too find primitive violence distressing,' agreed the Doctor. 'Especially when I'm on the receiving end!'

The Valeyard rose. 'I too find it repugnant, My lady. But the Doctor has a well-known predeliction for violence.'

The Doctor leaped to his feet. 'That is a foul slur!'

'Do not interrupt, Doctor,' commanded the Inquisitor.

The Doctor was not to be silenced. 'I am sorry, My Lady, but I am not given to violence as the Valeyard here suggests. Occasionally I may be forced to resort to a modicum of force—'

'Please be silent, Doctor,' interrupted the Inquisitor. 'You will be given ample opportunity to put your case at a later time. Valeyard, I would appreciate it if these brutal and repetitious scenes could be kept to a minimum.'

The Valeyard bowed. 'My Lady, it is certainly not my wish to cause you an unnecessary affront – but the accused's offences are such that a certain amount of graphic detail is unavoidable.'

The Inquisitor sighed. 'Very well. Continue!'

While the Doctor's party was being marched back through the woods towards the village, Merdeen was moving swiftly through the tunnels. Suddenly Grell appeared in front of him.

He was carrying a loaded hand-crossbow – and the weapon was aimed at Merdeen.

'You seem lost,' taunted Grell.

'Not I,' said Merdeen. 'Although you, Grell, seem to have mislaid your train.'

'Stealth is better achieved on foot – especially when we hunt dark secrets.'

'I thought we hunted the Doctor,' said Merdeen.

'Him too.'

Suddenly the voice of Drathro sounded in Merdeen's helmet.

'Merdeen!'

'Immortal?'

'I have urgent work for Balazar, but I cannot find him.'

'I will search for him at once, Immortal.'

Merdeen moved away. The crossbow in Grell's hand moved to cover him. 'Where are you going?'

'I am commanded by the Immortal to find Balazar. You will continue your search for the Doctor.'

Ignoring the crossbow, Merdeen moved away.

In the tunnel near the entrance the Service Robot suddenly whirred into life. Lurching a little, it moved away.

*

In the control room, Tandrell was jubilant. 'I did it. I reactivated the robot!'

'I think you'll find I did it,' sneered Humker.

'I did!'

'No, I did it!'

'Silence,' roared Drathro. 'You drain my energy reserve with your constant infantile bickering.'

His two assistants fell into a sulky silence.

Sitting on her carved wooden throne, before the altar of the Sacred Flame, a triumphant Queen Katryca surveyed her recovered captives. Her eye fastened on a cowering Glitz. 'So,' she said silkily, 'My hospitality was not to your liking?'

Glitz made a feeble attempt at a smile. 'Just needed to step out for a breath of air.'

Katryca looked curiously at her one new captive. 'And who is this?'

The Doctor beamed. 'How do you do? I am known as the Doctor. There's been a terrible mistake, I really shouldn't be here.'

Katryca studied him. 'Another Star Traveller?'

'In a manner of speaking,' said the Doctor modestly.

'And are you interested in the great totem of Haldron?'

'I beg your pardon?'

'She means the black-light convertor,' muttered Glitz.

'Ah, yes indeed,' said the Doctor. 'Now, how could you possibly have known that?'

Katryca turned to Broken Tooth. 'Has he been searched for guns?'

'He has none, Your Majesty,' said Broken Tooth.

'That makes you very unusual – for a Star Traveller, Doctor,' said Katryca. 'Especially one who is interested in the great totem.'

'I've come to repair it,' explained the Doctor.

'You are prompt, Doctor,' snapped Katryca. 'Your friends have only just damaged it!'

'Those are not my friends, Your Majesty. And your great totem is not what is seems.'

'Please explain.'

'Its function is to convert ultral-violet rays into black light . . .'

'Interesting,' said Katryca. 'Though I do not understand what you are saying.'

The Doctor said, 'Well, Drathro, the Immortal, depends on black light to function.'

Katryca said, 'Yet your friend here told me that the totem was a navigational beacon.'

'He lies,' said the Doctor.

Katryca nodded. 'It seems to be a common complaint amongst Star Travellers.'

'I am not a liar,' protested Glitz unconvincingly.

'How shall I know who lies and who speaks truth,' said Katryca. 'All I am certain of is that our gods are angered at your coming. I shall read their wishes in the flames.'

The Doctor turned to go. 'I'm sorry to appear discourteous, but I really must be getting back to Drathro—'

'Remain where you are!' ordered Katryca. The raised spears of her guards reinforced her words.

'You have no quarrel with us,' protested the Doctor. He waved towards Dibber and Glitz. 'They're the one's who destroyed your totem.'

'You are all Star Travellers,' said Katryca coldly. 'Star

78

Travelling is forbidden by the gods.' She pointed to Balazar, who bowed low. 'The underground dweller shall be accepted into our tribe. As for the rest – remove them from my sight!'

9

The Attack of the Robot

It had been a long and difficult task manoeuvering the Service Robot up to the Surface, but Humker and Tandrell had managed it at last.

Now the Robot was outside, trundling on its caterpillar tracks through the woods, en route to the native village.

What the robot saw through its vision circuitry was relayed onto the monitor screen.

Tandrell and Humker were surveying the results with distaste.

'All that unpleasant green,' said Humker.

'It is "vegetation",' said Tandrell.

Humker looked at the metal shape towering over them. 'Why was it not burned, Drathro?'

'Only part of the planet was consumed by fire.'

'But what is the function of this vegetation?' asked Humker.

'It supports primitive life,' rumbled Drathro.

'Primitive life is unnecessary,' said Tandrell fastidiously.

'So vegetation is unnecessary,' concluded Humker.

'Your syllogism is also unnecessary,' said Tandrell triumphantly.

Humker scowled. 'It is not a true syllogism, Tandrell.

It contained only the major and minor premiss.'

'It was still unnecessary,' said Tandrell petulantly. 'Like so much else that you say, Humker.'

'See,' said Humker, pointing to the monitor. The village wall and the group of stone dwellings beyond had just appeared on the screen.

The Doctor, Peri, Dibber and Glitz were marched into the prison hut by Broken Tooth and Balazar.

'Thought we'd seen the last of this place,' muttered Dibber.

'Look, Balazar,' said the Doctor urgently. 'You've got to help us get out of here.'

Balazar shrank back. 'I dare not, Doctor.'

Broken Tooth glanced uneasily at the guards outside the door. 'The Queen would burn us in your place if we helped you escape.'

'If I don't get out of here we'll all burn,' said the Doctor grimly.

Glitz scowled at him. 'Well, you're the Time Lord. Haven't you got a ring you can rub, or a magic lamp? Something for these little emergencies.'

'Hardly,' said the Doctor. 'More your style, I'd have thought. Anyway, what did bring you here?'

'Purely a private enterprise, Doctor,' said Glitz hurriedly. 'The collection of a few mouldering files, of no value except to scholars like myself.'

'I see. You're a scholarly philanthropist, are you?'

'My description exactly, Doctor!'

'Who goes around blowing up black-light convertors?' added the Doctor unkindly.

Glitz shrugged. 'A small expediency. If I am to endow

a library on my home planet of Salostopus—'

'In the constellation of Andromeda?' interrupted the Doctor.

'You know of it?'

The Doctor nodded.

'What we don't know,' said Peri, 'is the name of this planet.'

'You mean he hasn't told you?' Glitz gave the Doctor a reproachful look. 'A man of your learning – tut tut!' He turned to Peri. 'It's Earth, of course.'

Peri gave the Doctor a triumphant look. 'I said so, didn't I?'

'But it's in the wrong place,' protested the Doctor.

Glitz shrugged. 'Only by a couple of light years.'

'That's why the lost expedition missed it,' said Dibber.

'What lost expedition?'

'Andromeda bunged off these robots in a relief ship—'

'Don't prattle Dibber,' snapped Glitz. 'All that was a long time ago.'

Balazar cleared his throat. 'The word "Earth" is mentioned many times by that great writer HM Stationery Office.'

As no-one quite knew what to say to this, there was an awkward silence, finally broken by a shattering crash as the Service Robot smashed straight through the wall of the hut, showering rubble everywhere.

'I thought we'd seen the last of him as well,' said Dibber.

The robot stood swinging to and for as if uncertain what to do next.

'Shut up Dibber,' whispered Glitz, ducking behind his burly colleague for shelter. 'Stand in front of me where I can keep an eye on you.'

'Keep calm and stay still everyone,' said the Doctor quietly. 'It's looking for me, but I think it's still confused.'

Balazar and Broken Tooth were a little behind the Robot. They managed to slip through the open gap without being seen, but suddenly the robot got a fix on the Doctor and began advancing towards him.

'Can't you shake its hand or something?' suggested Glitz.

The Doctor stepped boldly forward. 'How do you do? I am known as the Doctor.'

He reached out and grasped an arm-like protrusion on the robot's casing – and received a shock that threw him clear across the hut.

Advancing on its victim, the robot extruded a number of steely, rope-like filaments. They whipped around the Doctor and dragged him towards the robot, lashing him to its casing in a sort of metallic spider's web.

Its victim firmly secured, the robot turned and trundled through the gap in the shattered wall.

'Now's our chance, Dibber,' said Glitz.

'We've got to help the Doctor,' screamed Peri.

'He'll be all right,' said Glitz soothingly. 'He's in good hands! Come on!'

'No!' protested Peri, but Glitz and Dibber dragged her away between them.

For the second time, Broken Tooth had the unhappy duty of telling Queen Katryca that she had lost her prisoners. 'Escaped? Again? I told you to guard them!'

'The Immortal came and took them,' said Balazar.

Katryca stared unbelievingly at him.

'We both saw him,' said Broken Tooth. 'He walked through the wall!'

Katryca leaped to her feet. 'Get the guns!' she ordered.

As the Service Robot moved away from the village, Drathro studied the monitor, brooding over the implications of what he had seen.

'Habitations! Only man makes habitations. All life on this planet perished in the fire. If men now live on the surface, they must have come from my biosphere. From here, underground...'

'How could that be?' said Humker, shocked.

'It is forbidden,' said Tandrell. 'All work-units obey your orders.' Drathro's deep voice was angry. 'Some must have escaped. They were helped to escape. That is what has happened.'

'They are not important,' said Humker.

'They are out of control' roared Drathro. 'Outside my plan.'

Tandrell nodded. 'They are outlaws.'

'Now my existence is threatened,' boomed Drathro. 'They have destroyed the source of my energy. We must take measures. Create a defensive system. Identify and destroy the traitors!'

Drathro was becoming paranoid.

In the Courtroom, the Doctor rose in indignation. 'All this is irrelevant and hypothetical.'

'Background testimony,' snapped the Valeyard.

'What possible value does the ... farmyard here think there is in listening to a half-incapacitated robot, and a couple of diminuitive nitwits?'

'You are allowing your disrespect to show again, Doctor,' said the Inquisitor icily.

'I'm sorry, My Lady. But the question still stands.'

'The Valeyard has the right to include any evidence he considers relevant – provided he can justify its inclusion.'

'But surely,' said the Doctor, 'any record relating to persons not in my presence must be sheer conjecture?'

The Valeyard rose. 'The accused is clearly ignorant of the latest methods of surveillance, My Lady.'

The Inquisitor turned towards the Doctor. 'This evidence is taken from the Matrix – a knowledge bank fed constantly by the experiences of all Time Lords, wherever they may be.'

'Yes, yes, yes,' said the Doctor impatiently. 'I know that. My whole point is – I'm not!'

She stared at him in exasperation. 'Not what?'

'Not present,' said the Doctor. 'Not part of the scenes being presented by the scrapyard, sorry, sorry, force of habit, the Valeyard here.'

The Valeyard gave a superior smile. 'Ah but Doctor, the experiences of third parties can also be monitored and accessed if needed – as long as they are in the collection range of a TARDIS.'

The Doctor looked nonplussed. 'Indeed? But my TARDIS is an old model. Are you telling me it's been bugged – without my knowledge?'

'Bugged?' The Inquisitor was baffled.

'A reference, apparently, to the new surveillance system,' explained the Valeyard. 'The Doctor is using an

Earth term.'

The Inquisitor was becoming impatient. 'I think we are wasting time on an unimportant issue. Continue, Valeyard.'

The Robot trundled through the forest, the Doctor lashed to its casing by a steel cocoon.

A large party of warriors appeared in the woods ahead. It was led by Broken Tooth, and by Queen Katryca herself.

Both carried laser rifles. Many of the others also carried guns, weapons taken from certain unfortunate Star Travellers in years gone by.

'Stop Immortal!' roared Katryca.

Like the rest of her people, she had assumed that the robot that had attacked them was the Immortal of whom escapees from the underground had spoken – not realizing that the real Immortal was a far more formidable proposition.

The Service Robot ignored her.

Raising her rifle, Katryca opened fire.

Broken Tooth followed, and a ragged volley of laser-bolts and projectiles hummed around the robot. Some of them actually hit it, more by luck than skill.

The robot staggered, then lurched forward with its living cargo as the tribesmen fired again and again. From a nearby hillock Dibber and Glitz watched with detached interest while Peri, held firmly between them, looked on in agonized concern.

'They'll kill the Doctor,' she shrieked.

'We've all got to go some time,' said Glitz philosophically.

'You're all heart,' said Peri bitterly.

'The supreme sacrifice – and all for us,' said Glitz admiringly. 'What a person. If I have time I shall compose the eulogy for his funeral.'

There was another ragged volley and another. Smoke streaked from the robot's casing. It lurched forwards a few more yards, and then toppled slowly over.

Drathro and his assistants watched the battle on the monitor – until, that is, the picture lurched dizzily and the screen went blank.

The scenes they had witnessed provided fresh fuel for Drathro's paranoid fears. 'They have guns. From where?'

'Guns can be manufactured,' said Humker.

'Indeed,' said Tandrell. 'But their manufacture requires advanced technology.'

'The fact that they have guns means they also have advanced technology.'

'False reasoning, Humker,' said Tandrell. 'They are savages. Therefore their guns must have been supplied from without.'

Humker glanced at the blank screen. 'The Service Robot has ceased to function.'

'On our present data, that is the logical conclusion,' agreed Tandrell.

'It is obvious. It has ceased transmitting signals.'

'The Doctor is from Gallifrey,' rumbled Drathro in his deep mechanical-sounding tones. 'He has been sent to recover the secrets left by the Sleepers. To do that, he has armed the outlaws. He intends to foment rebellion against my authority.'

Tandrell put his head close to Humker's and whispered, 'And with nothing left here but the power from a few back-up storage cells, he's quite likely to succeed.'

'Then what will happen to us?' whispered Humker.

Tandrell looked at him. 'I dread to think...'

For some time Merdeen had suspected he was being followed. He ducked suddenly into an alcove and waited.

Grell came along the corridor, crossbow in hand.

Drawing his own weapon, Merdeen stepped forward to confront him. 'Are you following me?'

'Like you I'm looking for a lost man. It occurred to me that it might prove more productive if we worked as a team.'

Merdeen said suspiciously, 'What makes you think the Doctor and Balazar will be together?'

'Events,' said Grell mysteriously.

'Meaning?'

'I don't think the Immortal's orders are always carried out,' said Grell. 'Especially when it comes to Culling.'

'I always supervise the Culls myself,' said Merdeen calmly.

'I know.'

'Then what are you suggesting, Grell?'

'I think you send people outside.'

Concealing his shock Merdeen said casually, 'Then they are destroyed by the Fire. Does it matter how they die?'

'That depends if you really believe that the surface of the planet still burns.'

'I believe what the Immortal tells me,' said Merdeen.

'I believe you are a liar,' said Grell calmly. 'The Doctor is with Balazar, isn't he? And both have left the subways!'

'Then why does the Immortal order us to search for them?'

'I don't know,' said Grell. 'But I really think we ought to talk about all this, Merdeen.' He paused. 'Unless, of course, you would prefer that I took my suspicions to the Immortal...'

10

Hunt for the Doctor

The awe-stricken villagers gathered about the toppled robot, unable to believe what they had achieved.

None of them paid the slightest attention to the body of the Doctor, half hidden beneath the still smouldering robot.

'Is the Immortal dead at last?' whispered Balazar.

Katryca said proudly. 'The Immortal's reign is ended!'

A ragged cheer went up, led by the faithful Broken Tooth. 'Katryca the Great One! Long Live Queen Katryca!'

Balazar said wonderingly. 'Now the Immortal is dead, how shall men live?'

'In the Tribe of the Free we had no need of the Immortal,' said Katryca proudly. 'We shall live as we have always lived. And now the Immortal's secrets shall be ours.'

'How?' asked Broken Tooth.

'Do you not see, Broken Tooth? They are ours for the taking.'

'The Immortal's castle?' said Balazar.

'Yes,' said Katryca exultantly. 'It is ours now. All the tools, the metal, the strange materials that bend but do not break... All the mysteries and treasures of our forefathers that we shall learn to use again. Are we agreed?'

There was a rumble of assent.

'Then we attack!' screamed Katryca.

She set off for the tunnel entrance, her warriors streaming after her.

As soon as they had disappeared into the trees, Glitz and Dibber allowed Peri to pull free. She ran to kneel beside the Doctor who lay very still, his face a ghastly white.

'Doctor,' she sobbed 'Doctor, please...'

Dibber and Glitz ambled up and looked down at her.

'I'm afraid he's a gonner,' said Glitz. 'You can always tell by the colour.'

Dibber nodded. 'Definitely a stiff, Mr Glitz.'

'Help me get the robot off him,' pleaded Peri.

'I shouldn't bother,' said Glitz. 'Even if he's alive, he's probably got horrible injuries.'

'That's right,' said Dibber. 'Those Ensen guns blow you all to bits.'

They turned and strolled away through the trees.

'Talking of guns, Dibber,' said Glitz, as soon as they were out of Peri's sight, 'we need the heavy artillery, which, if memory serves me, is hidden not a million miles from this spot.'

Dibber nodded. 'Good idea of mine to bring the multi-blasters, eh, Mr Glitz?'

Glitz rubbed his hands together. 'I'll teach that two-faced harridan and her bunch of ignorant peasants to trifle with Sabalom Glitz!'

'They've all gone down the tunnels now,' Dibber pointed out.

'So we'll blow them out through the roof,' snarled Glitz. '—if the robot doesn't get them first!'

'Let's get them then,' said Dibber.

Glitz put a hand on his arm. 'No, you get them, Dibber. I'll meet you by the entrance.'

'Those multi-blasters weigh at least—'

Glitz held up his hand. 'Exactly. That's why I employ you Dibber. To fetch and carry. Now cut along, there's a good lad...'

Dibber gave him a suspicious look, then turned away towards the place where the guns were hidden.

Glitz set off for the tunnel entrance at an ungainly run

Peri struggled hard to heave the Doctor from beneath the bulk of the robot but he remained obstinately stuck. Suddenly he groaned and opened his eyes.

'You're alive,' gasped Peri. 'I knew it.'

'My head hurts abominably, Sarah Jane,' complained the Doctor feebly. 'Where are we?'

'I'm not Sarah Jane, I'm Peri! And you're lying under the remains of a robot!'

Oh yes, I remember now.' He tried to get up and failed. 'Get this thing off me!'

'I've been trying to!'

Between them they managed to shift the metal bulk of the robot sufficiently to enable the Doctor to roll free.

He scrambled to his feet. 'Where are Katryca and the others?'

'They've gone underground.'

'Whatever for?'

'From what I could hear, now Katryca's killed the Immortal she's planning a takeover.'

The Doctor looked at the toppled robot. 'That? That's not the Immortal, it's just a Service Robot. How long have they been gone?'

'Just a few minutes.'

'We'd better go after them.'

'Why?'

'They've got to be stopped. The situation is worse than you imagine.'

'It always is,' said Peri wearily.

The Doctor was already on his way and Peri hurried after him.

Katryca led her little army through the first tunnel, down the long steps to the lower one, then up to the door that led to the lower levels.

'How does the great door open?' demanded Katryca.

Broken Tooth pointed to the handle. 'You turn this.'

'Open it!'

Broken Tooth obeyed, and the door slid open.

Katryca handed her gun to a startled Balazar. 'You and Broken Tooth have lived in this blackness. You will lead the way.'

Broken Tooth said, 'I know a tunnel which leads straight to the Immortal's castle.'

'Forward!' ordered Katryca.

Nervously the tribesmen filed through the door.

Their entrance was observed on the control room monitor screen.

'They look very fierce,' said Humker.

'Naturally,' said Tandrell. 'They live as wild creatures.'

'They are coming towards us,' Humker pointed out.

'You have a gift for the obvious, Humker.'

'Surely they will not attack us?'

'That is clearly their intention.'

'I do not understand the logic,' protested Humker. 'We have not harmed them.'

'It is Rebellion,' said Drathro heavily.

'What shall we do if they break in?' asked Humker.

Drathro said, 'I shall kill them.'

Tandrell said, 'Their guns destroyed your Service Robot, Drathro.'

'My plating is stronger,' boomed Drathro. 'My circuits are well protected. Their guns will only kill you.'

'But if we die,' said Humker hurriedly, 'Who will assist with your research?'

'The Doctor,' said Drathro, and turned away.

Broken Tooth stopped the invading party at a tunnel junction. 'Halt!'

They halted.

'I fear the worst,' said Broken Tooth gloomily.

'What is wrong?' asked Katryca. 'Are we lost?'

Broken Tooth nodded sadly. 'Marb Station is back this way.'

'It is forward,' said Balazar confidently. 'And thence to the castle of the Immortal.'

'We must have no indecision in the Tribe of the Free,' shouted Katryca. 'Long have we waited for this moment. The Immortal is dead and we shall plunder his castle. The spoils of triumph are ours. Now – *which way is it*?'

'This way,' shouted Broken Tooth and Balazar in unison.

Balazar pointed forward, and Broken Tooth back.

'Am I surrounded by fools?' shrieked Katryca. 'We

shall go forward!'

'But Katryca,' protested Broken Tooth.

'Forward, I say! I have read it in the flames, many times. We go forward!'

A flashing arc of electricity sizzled through the console that the Doctor had dismantled.

'That is not correct,' said Humker suspiciously.

Tandrell sighed. 'There is clearly a mechanical defect.'

'An electronic malfunction,' said Humker sagely.

Tandrell nodded. 'Perhaps the Doctor created the problem?'

Humker turned to their master. 'Have you seen this, Drathro?'

Drathro came over to them. To their horror he staggered a little and his voice was blurred.

'I do not need to. My condition tells me of the failure of the black-light system.'

'What can have caused it?' asked Humker.

'There were no warning signs,' said Tandrell.

'It was accelerated by the destruction of the black-light convertor,' said Drathro thickly.

'Destruction?' breathed Tandrell.

'The Service Robot relayed the information as it entered the village.'

'Can we not repair it?' suggested Tandrell hopefully.

Drathro's voice dragged wearily. 'No. Soon the black-light system will collapse in upon itself, and we shall all cease to function.'

Drathro sounded resigned to his fate.

*

The Doctor and Peri were hurrying along one of the lower tunnels.

'The trouble is, his refraction dipoles are worn out,' said the Doctor. 'Nothing for it now but to shut the whole black light system down.'

'That sounds simple enough,' said Peri hopefully.

'Oh, it is. But if I shut the system down I shut Drathro down as well, and I can't see him agreeing to that!'

'So what happens if he won't let you?'

'Then the black-light system will explode and destroy everything in these tunnels.'

'Oh great. So that's why we're going in?'

'I can't let people die, Peri,' said the Doctor soberly. 'Not if there's a chance of saving them.'

They hurried on.

Glitz was waiting by the entrance as Dibber staggered up with the two multi-blasters, weapons that were a sort of portable laser-cannon. 'You got the guns then?'

'Looks like it, Mr Glitz.'

'I tell you something funny Dibber. I popped back to check on the Doctor. We was wrong about him. He's bunked off.'

'He hasn't bunked off, Mr Glitz. He's gone down below. I caught a glimpse of him from a distance. He has Peri with him.'

'So he is after the same as we are then!'

'Could be.'

'Course he is,' said Glitz confidently. 'I knew it all along. He's got no more interest in the scientific side than I have!'

'You didn't fool him saying you was a philatelist, Mr

Glitz.'

'Philanthropist, you ignorant dink. Why, don't I look like one then?'

'How do I know, I've never seen one.'

'A philanthropist, my son, is someone who gives away all their Grotzis, out of the simple goodness of their hearts.'

'Oh, you mean they're stupid? Yeah, well maybe you do look like one then.'

Glitz grabbed one of the guns. 'Get down that hole, Dibber. Oh dear, these things are heavy, aren't they?'

When they reached the top of the steep steps, Glitz made a vain attempt to get Dibber to carry both guns. Dibber ignored him.

'Please Dibber,' begged Glitz as he staggered down the steps after him.'

'You always did despise muscle,' said Dibber reprovingly.

'Not when there are heavy things to carry lad. Anyway, Dibber, if we should run into the Doctor again—'

'We shoot him?'

They descended the steps and made for the door that led to the lower levels.

'Not a bad idea lad,' said Glitz. 'But whatever you do, don't open your big parlo and let him know we're after the stuff...'

On the Courtroom screen the remainder of Glitz's words became a series of beeps, and the picture went black.

The Inquisitor raised her eyebrows.

'The remainder of that evidence has been excised, My Lady,' said the Valeyard smoothly.

'Excised?'

'By order of the High Council.'

'This is a judicial enquiry, appointed by the High Council, but independently conducted.' The Inquisitor's tone was one of quiet fury. 'It is *my* duty, Valeyard, to determine what evidence is relevant.'

'Of course, My Lady. The High Council simply felt that certain areas of testimony should not be revealed.'

'And why not?'

'It was judged to be against the public interest, My Lady.'

'I cannot conduct a full and searching enquiry without full access to the evidence,' said the Inquisitor flatly.

'Naturally, My Lady, the High Council would be prepared to let you consider the full record *in camera*.'

'In secret? But that would be unfair to the defendant. Do you wish to lodge a formal objection at this time, Doctor?'

The Doctor sat back, considering. At last he said, 'No, My Lady. Let the Valeyard continue. Let's give him enough rope to hang himself.'

'Very well, Doctor. Proceed, Valeyard.'

The Valeyard shot the Doctor a quick glance, before turning back to the screen. To the Doctor's huge delight, he saw that somehow he'd got the Valeyard worried.

It was the first chink in the Valeyard's armour.

'Hurry Peri,' said the Doctor. 'There isn't much time.'

'How long before this black-light thing goes up?'

'There's no telling. We've just got to get past Katryca, into the Castle, and make that demented robot see sense.'

Suddenly Merdeen stepped from an alcove. The crossbow gun in his hand was aimed at the Doctor. 'So you have returned, Doctor.'

'Missed your train, Merdeen?'

'The train is noisy, Doctor. We hunt best on foot.'

'Oh? And what are you hunting?'

'You, Doctor,' said Merdeen.

He raised the crossbow-gun and fired at point-blank range.

11

Secrets

Merdeen's crossbow bolt wasn't aimed at the Doctor.

It was directed at Grell, who had emerged from another alcove, his crossbow aimed at the Doctor's back. But Merdeen had fired first. Grell crashed to the ground, a crossbow bolt in his breast.

Merdeen ran to the body and knelt beside it. 'Why Grell?' he whispered. 'Why?'

'You betrayed...' said Grell feebly. His voice tailed away.

'No,' said Merdeen passionately. 'We were not meant to live like this. We should be free...' he looked up at the Doctor. 'He wanted the glory of your capture, to please the Immortal.'

'Don't blame yourself, Merdeen.'

'I've known him all his life,' said Merdeen brokenly, as he got to his feet. 'I asked for him to join the guards. I hoped one day he might see there was no reason for the Cullings.'

'Perhaps I can convince the Immortal of that,' said the Doctor urgently. 'I must get in to his Castle.'

'He will kill you,' said Merdeen dully.

'Not if he thinks I can still be of use to him. Come on, Merdeen, there isn't much time...'

*

Drathro stood swaying in the centre of his malfunctioning control room. Lights flashed wildly on the consoles and electricity arced across them.

'The black-light system will soon collapse in on itself,' he said in a blurred, dragging voice. 'Then we shall all cease to function.'

As Drathro moved away, Tandrell whispered, 'We must leave here, Humker.'

'Where could we go?'

'I don't know. But Drathro says there will be an explosion and we shall all be killed. So, the logical course is to leave.'

Humker glanced up at the monitor and saw a ragged-looking group of armed men pounding down the corridor, a red-haired woman leading them.

'The wild ones!' said Humker. 'We are too late.'

'I've always said you talked too much,' said Tandrell. 'Come on!'

He led the way to the door.

By now Katryca and her little army were literally battering at the Castle doors. But their gun butts and spear handles made no impression.

'The gates will not yield, Katryca,' said Broken Tooth gloomily. 'They are of iron.'

'Then we will cut down the walls,' said Katryca, undeterred. 'Fetch tools!'

'Wait,' called Balazar. 'The Castle gates open.'

As they watched the gates swung slowly open.

Katryca turned to rally her reluctant warriors. 'Come, the Immortal is dead. We have nothing to fear!'

She led them across the anteroom towards the inner

doors. When the warriors had all passed through, Humker and Tandrell slipped out from behind the doors and disappeared down the corridor. As the little army crossed the anteroom, the inner doors opened also. Excitedly they hurried into the control room, Katryca and Broken Tooth in the lead.

Drathro was waiting for them. They stared up at the gleaming metal figure with its strange sickle-shaped head in horrified amazement.

'It can't be,' whispered Katryca.

But somehow they all knew that this was the true Immortal.

'Why have you entered here?' boomed Drathro in his slurred, dragging voice.

Katryca's courage did not fail her. 'The guns, Broken Tooth!'

'Lay aside your useless toys,' ordered Drathro. 'I ask why have you entered here?'

'We are the tribe of the Free.'

'You are vassals,' said Drathro contemptuously. 'Outside the law, outside the Plan. You have brought disorder where order reigned.'

Broken Tooth raised his gun, and Drathro lashed out and shattered it in his hand.

'I am Katryca, Queen of the—'

Drathro's clamplike hand fastened about her throat. For a second or two the whole robot pulsed with power.

Katryca writhed and twisted for a moment, then her charred body dropped to the ground, face blackened and hair scorched away. Broken Tooth launched himself at the robot in a mad frenzy. Drathro's other hand clamped about his throat. Seconds later his twisted body dropped beside that of his Queen, his features scorched beyond all recognition.

'You cause me to waste energy,' said Drathro reprovingly. 'Wait outside all of you. You will be Culled in accordance with the Plan.'

'Oh great Immortal one,' cried Balazar.

Drathro dismissed him. 'Go. Do not attempt to hide. My guards will track you down.'

Balazar led the defeated army from the control room.

Humker and Tandrell hurried along the corridors.

'I remember these subways from my childhood,' said Humker.

'Is this then the way to the surface?'

'I said I remembered the subways, Tandrell – not where they led!'

'If we do not find the surface, Drathro's guards will find us.'

'First we must deal with the wild ones. Then if there is an explosion . . .'

They turned a corner and ran straight into the Doctor, Peri and Merdeen.

'Tumker and Handrail,' said the Doctor. 'Where are you two off to?'

'We are leaving, Doctor, said Humker.

'Drathro says there is going to be an explosion,' said Tandrell.

'I know,' said the Doctor ruefully.

'It is a mechanical fault, said Tandrell.

'Electronic,' insisted Humker.

Tandrell said worriedly, 'There is a constant electrical discharge from one pole to another.'

'Then I may only have minutes,' said the Doctor

worriedly. 'Come on!'

The Doctor and his party hurried away.

Sitting back in the Courtroom the Doctor said, 'I didn't appear to be hurrying there, did I? But that deceptively easy gait of mine covers the ground at amazing speed.'

'I did not interrupt the evidence to compliment you on your athleticism, Doctor,' said the Inquisitor coldly.

The Doctor looked crestfallen. 'Oh well, you can if you like. All compliments gratefully accepted.'

'May I remind you yet again that this is a serious trial?'

The Doctor sprang to his feet. 'It is not serious, it is a farce,' he said furiously. 'A farrago of trumped-up charges.'

'You will have the opportunity in due course to rebut any or all of the Valeyard's charges, Doctor.'

The Doctor laughed scornfully. 'The Valeyard's charges! I always thought Valeyard meant Learned Court Prosecutor.'

'And so it does,' said the Valeyard stiffly.

'Not in your case, sir,' said the Doctor witheringly. 'Your points of law are spurious, your evidence weak, verging on the irrelevant, and your reasoning quite unsound. In fact, your point of view belongs in quite another place. Perhaps the mantle of Valeyard was a mistake. I would therefore suggest that you change it for the garment of quite another sort of yard – that of a knacker's yard! Your arguments are as tried and worn out as the poor unfortunates that end up there.'

Having got all this off his chest the Doctor sat down again, feeling very much better.

The Inquisitor was furious. 'You will apologize at

once, Doctor!'

The Doctor leaped to his feet again. 'For telling the truth? Never!' He sat down again.

The Valeyard rose. 'The Doctor is well known for his childish outbursts. I do not find the ramblings of an immature mind offensive.'

'Immature?' the Doctor was outraged.

'It is that particular state of mind that has made it necessary for you to be brought before this Court.'

'Immature!' said the Doctor again. 'I was on Ravolox trying to avert a catastrophe – the death of several hundred innocent people. Surely not even in the eyes of the Time Lords can that be deemed immature – or a crime!'

'The crime was in being there, Doctor,' said the Valeyard. 'Your immaturity lay in not realizing that you had broken a cardinal law of the Time Lords. Your presence initiated the whole chain of events which we have witnessed.'

'Thank you, Valeyard,' said the Inquisitor. 'It was just that point concerning the relevance of the evidence that I had intended to raise.'

The Valeyard bowed. 'My pleasure, Inquisitor.'

The Doctor threw himself back in his chair. 'Oh this is ridiculous!'

'May we continue?' asked the Inquisitor pointedly. 'I tire of this empty banter.'

The Valeyard bowed again. 'Of course, My Lady.'

The Doctor and Peri hurried up to the Castle gates – and stopped in astonishment at the sight of the sorry-looking group of warriors, now disarmed, bunched under guard outside.

The Doctor went up to Balazar. 'What happened?'

'Alas, Doctor, these are woeful times for the Tribe of the Free. The Queen is dead! The Immortal struck her down with a bolt of lightning.'

'Where is he now?'

'The All-Powerful One is in his Castle.'

'Why did he let you go?' asked Peri.

'We are waiting to be Culled,' said Balazar sadly.

'You'll be Culled all right,' said the Doctor grimly. 'And so will everybody else around here if I don't get into that Castle.' He marched up to the gates. 'Drathro, this is the Doctor. Let me in at once, do you hear me?'

'It's no good Doctor,' said Merdeen. 'You can only speak to the Immortal through the communication box.'

The Doctor sighed. 'I forgot. Doesn't exactly entertain a lot, does he? Right, quickly Merdeen, take me to the nearest one.'

Dibber and Glitz came creeping around the corner of the tunnels, bowed down by the weight of their multi-blasters.

'When we find this Castle,' began Dibber.

Gasping, Glitz put down his multi-blaster. 'Dibber, I must rest. I am exhausted.'

'If we find this Castle,' Dibber went on, 'and knock out the L3 robot – how are we ever going to find these secrets you keep on about?'

'Dibber, would I have spent all this time and effort – not to mention a small fortune – if I wasn't certain on that point?'

'Yeah, but even if we do find 'em they might not be

106

worth anything. Not after five hundred years.'

'Do me a favour, Dibber,' said Glitz wearily. 'The Sleepers found a way into—'

On the Courtroom screen, Glitz's final words had been carefully bleeped out.

The Doctor sprang to his feet. 'What is going on?'

'That question had formed in my own mind, Doctor,' said the Inquisitor. 'Well, Valeyard?'

12

Tradesman's Entrance

The Valeyard remained calm beneath the accusing stares of both the Doctor and the Inquisitor.

'The information that has been extracted is for your eyes and ears only, My Lady.'

'Something else it is not in the public interest to reveal?'

'Exactly so, My Lady.'

'This is a charade,' said the Doctor. 'If that information was known to those two rogues, what possible reason can there be for concealing it from this Court?'

'This trial is concerned only with your actions, Doctor, and their consequences,' said the Valeyard. 'Wider issues – if there are any – are not within our terms of reference.'

The Inquisitor was far from pleased. 'Perhaps that is something I should decide, Valeyard.'

'Of course, My Lady. My own instructions were to pursue only matters pertinent to the central issue.'

There was a long pause. Then the Inquisitor said, 'That is accepted. However, I should like to hear that section again.'

*

'Do me a favour, Dibber,' said Glitz wearily. 'The sleepers found a way into the (*word bleeped*) the biggest net of information in the universe. So you think they were nicking recipes for making chutney?'

'Yeah, but do we know what these secrets are?'

'Facts, my son,' said Glitz impressively. 'Figures and formulas. Travelling faster than light, anti-gravity power. Dimensional transference. Scientific stuff like that. Worth a fortune.'

'How?'

'We sell it, Dibber. A government here, a federation there. They're all in the market for that sort of high-tech cobblers.' He heaved his gun up again. 'Don't think about it, Dibber. 'You'll give yourself a hernia...'

Dibber picked up his multi-blaster and they went on their way.

The Doctor and Peri stood watching while Merdeen tried unsuccessfully to operate the communications box.

'The Immortal does not always answer,' said Merdeen apologetically.

Suddenly Drathro's voice, feebler than usual but quite unmistakable, crackled from the apparatus. 'Yes, Merdeen?'

'You commanded me to find the Doctor, Immortal. I have him here.'

The Doctor stepped into the field of the camera lens. 'I have returned to help you, Drathro.'

There was a long silence, then Drathro's voice said, 'You are too late.'

'If I believed that, I would not be here.'

'You are here because Merdeen found you.'

'No Drathro, I came voluntarily. There may yet be time to repair the black-light system.'

Another agonizing pause. Then Drathro said, 'Very well, Doctor. Present yourself at my portals – alone. Merdeen?'

'Yes, Immortal.'

Assemble my guards and cull all the organics who stand waiting outside my Castle.'

'At once, Immortal.'

Merdeen bowed and they hurried away.

The Doctor sprinted ahead to the Castle gates, while Peri and Balazar walked back more slowly with Merdeen.

'You can't do it, Merdeen,' urged Peri. 'You can't kill all those innocent people.'

'Peri is right,' said Balazar. You have seen the truth. It would be murder to kill them. 'You cannot do it.'

'Nor can I free them,' said Merdeen sadly. He knew that the bulk of the guards were still loyal to the Immortal.

'Well, just leave them,' pleaded Peri. 'Leave them for the present anyway.'

'The Immortal will kill me,' said Merdeen.

Peri said, 'If the Doctor's right we're all in danger anyway. We might all die.'

The outer and inner gates opened for the Doctor and soon he was back with Drathro in his control room.

The Doctor studied the erractically flickering console and shook his head. 'Well, I don't need a computer to tell me that system is defunct. I must shut it down.'

'No,' rumbled Drathro. 'You will not shut it down!'

'But it's the only way.'

'If the system is shut down, I too will cease.'

'But if it's allowed to run wild and heat to termination point, you'll cease then anyway, Drathro, and so will everyone and everything else around here.'

'That does not matter, Doctor. Everything here is my creation.'

'But there are several hundred people here, Drathro.'

'The work-units exist only to serve me. Without me they would have no function.'

'You can't see beyond your tin nose, can you,' said the Doctor exasperatedly.

'Is that abuse, Doctor?'

The Doctor made a mighty effort to keep calm. Robots responded to logic, not emotion. 'Listen, Drathro . . .'

'I am listening, Doctor.'

'Drathro, you are only a robot. Those people out there, the work-units, the organics, whatever you call them, are living creatures. They have a right to their lives.'

'Explain, why?'

The Docor sighed. 'I don't think I can, not in your terms. Whoever programmed you forgot to include moral values.'

'I understand values, Doctor. Is it your claim that organics are of greater value than robots?'

'Yes, if you care to look at it that way.'

'Then why should I be in command of organics?'

'You shouldn't. Without organics, there would be no robots, no one to create them.'

'Accepted,' said Drathro triumphantly. 'This proves that robots are more advanced than organics, therefore of greater value.'

111

The Doctor buried his head in his hands.

'Is there another way into the Castle, Merdeen?' demanded Peri. 'A back door or something.'

He shook his head. 'There are only the big doors.'

'There must be some other way in. The Doctor may need help. I've got to get in there.'

'There's the ration chute,' said Balazar.

'Ration chute?'

'Of course,' said Merdeen. 'Every day the Immortal sends out food to the work units. The chute must lead into the Castle.'

'Merdeen, you're a pal,' said Peri. 'You're both pals. Now, lead me to this chute.'

The Doctor was still continuing his extraordinary debate. He knew he had no chance of overcoming Drathro physically. He just had to win him over.

Robots were logical beings, and the course the Doctor was advocating was strictly logical. Surely Drathro must understand?

'Your trouble is, Drathro,' said the Doctor, 'you have no real concept of what life is!'

'I have studied my work-units for five centuries, Doctor. I understand all their responses.'

'Understanding isn't knowing, Drathro. Your work-units are the result of millions of years of development. Life!'

'I understand evolution.'

'But you don't. If you understood anything of what life was about, you would want to help me save those people out there.'

'But why. Doctor? I have said that without me they have no purpose.'

'Everything in life has purpose, Drathro. Every creature plays its part. The purpose of life is too big to be knowable. A million computers couldn't solve that one.'

'This discussion is of no value,' said Drathro dismissively. 'I do not wish my work-units to continue when I have ceased to function.'

'Oh, so that's it, is it,' said the Doctor softly. 'Hubris!'

'Hubris!? What is hubris?'

'Overwhelming arrogance. Insolent conceit. A human sin. You've controlled your pointless little empire far too long. Now you can't see anything beyond it.'

Dibber and Glitz were studying the Castle doors.

'We'll have to blast through them, Dibber.'

'Don't like it, Mr Glitz.'

'Why not? Five rounds rapid should do the trick.'

'What if the L3 robot is still functioning? And what if he's got an emergency backup support system?'

Glitz frowned. 'There's a lot of "What ifs" in there, lad!'

'Yeah, I know, said Dibber. 'And the most important of all is, what if I'm right?'

Glitz rubbed his chin. 'Maybe there's some kind of back way...'

Peri, Merdeen and Balazar were surveying a hatchway set into a tunnel wall.

'Are you sure this leads into the Castle?' asked Peri.

'It must do,' said Merdeen.

Balazar nodded. 'There's nowhere else for it to go.'

The hatchway was smeared with some kind of vegetable guck.

Peri looked at it dubiously. 'Talk about a tradesman's entrance . . .'

Glitz and Dibber came round the corner, laser cannons in their hands, covering the little group.

'Well, well,' said Glitz amiably.

'Glitz and Dibber,' said Peri. 'I wondered where you two had got to!'

'Where's your friend the Doctor?' asked Glitz.

'In the Castle,' said Peri.

Glitz gave Dibber a look. 'Didn't hang about, did he?'

'I'm worried about him, said Peri.

'So am I,' said Glitz.

Peri pointed to the hatch. 'Merdeen and Balazar think we can get into the Castle through this hatch.'

Glitz waved her onwards with his laser-cannon. 'Go on, then!'

Reluctantly Peri started to clamber through . . .

13

The Big Bang

The Doctor took an anguished look at the shuddering console. 'It may only be a matter of minutes, Drathro. Can't I make you see sense?'

'It is finished, Doctor.'

'Look,' said the Doctor desperately. 'It's not just this planet. Nobody knows what a black-light explosion can do, there's never been one.'

'There will be one soon.'

'Some people think it might set off a chain reaction which would roll on till all matter in the galaxy is exhausted. Is that what you want?'

'It is no longer of concern to me, Doctor.'

'Others believe an explosion of black light would cause dimensional transference – and that would threaten the stability of the entire universe!' The Doctor was shouting now.

Drathro ignored him. He was studying a monitor with a warning light flashing above it.

The monitor showed a group of figures emerging into a food storage tank, its walls still dripping with green vegetable slime. They moved across it and climbed into an enormous tube, that gave passage to the next chamber.

'Intruders in the food-production machinery,'

rumbled Drathro.

The Doctor stared at the monitor. 'That's Peri! And Merdeen, and Dibber and Glitz. What on earth are they up to?'

Drathro at least had no doubts. 'So that was your intention, Doctor.'

'What?'

'To distract me, while your friends attacked.'

Drathro moved to a sub console and began setting controls.

Suddenly the Doctor realized what he was doing. The robot was about to set the food-processing machinery into operation – with Peri and the others still inside.

'You can't do that,' shouted the Doctor.

He hurled himself on the robot in a vain attempt to drag it away. Drathro sent him flying across the control room with a casual swat.

Then the robot touched a control . . .

Suddenly the door at the end of the giant tube slid closed. From the other end an enormous whirling blade, its circumference exactly that of the tunnel, began sliding towards them. With a sick feeling, Peri realized that the tube was a kind of giant blender in which vegetables of all kinds were reduced to the green slime they'd seen on the walls. Now something very similar was going to happen to them . . .

Suddenly heat rays began bombarding the interior of the tube. The vegetables weren't just minced, and shredded, they were cooked as well!'

The enormous blade came nearer and nearer, reducing the space in which they could stand . . .

•

The Doctor staggered to his feet. He staggered to the monitor and saw what was happening to his friends.

'No!' he shouted again, and made a second, equally futile attempt to distract the robot.

Once again it smashed him aside, and he lay half-stunned.

Inside the tube they had very little time.

'What are we going to do?' yelled Peri. 'If we're not ground to death, we'll be fried!'

'Stand back,' grunted Dibber.

With a mighty effort he raised his laser-cannon, and blasted the side clean out of the tube.

Balazar, who had elected to stay behind as look-out, was peering into the hatch.

'What's happening?' he yelled.

He heard a series of explosions – and suddenly an enormous ball of green vegetable gunk shot from the hatchway, covering him from head to foot in green slime...

Dibber stumbled though the smoking hole in the wall into Drathro's control room. Immediately the robot smashed the laser cannon from his hands.

Glitz, who came next, dropped his weapon at once. 'We come in peace,' he said unconvincingly.

Peri and Merdeen staggered in after them.

'Are you all right, Doctor?' said Peri.

The Doctor got stiffly to his feet. 'For the moment,' he said grimly, his eyes on the still-vibrating black-light console. 'Though not for long, I fear!'

Drathro surveyed his prisoners. 'I could kill you all now, but there is no necessity. We are waiting for something the Doctor tells me is quite unique – a black-light explosion.'

'Do something, Dibber,' groaned Glitz.

'Like what?'

The Doctor said, 'I've been trying to convince this mobile junk heap here that none of this needs happen – if he'd let me shut the system down.'

'Seems eminently sensible to me,' said Glitz.

'Ah, but he won't listen to anything sensible,' said the Doctor bitterly. 'He needs black light to function, you see, so he sees no reason why the rest of us should survive. That is your narrowly egotistical little view, isn't it, Drathro?'

'If I am doomed, you are all doomed,' said the robot implacably.

The black-light console was juddering as if it would shake loose from the control-room floor, its lights flashing wildly.

It couldn't last much longer, thought the Doctor.

'Now, look here, wait a minute,' said Glitz. 'I mean, if it's only black light you want Drathro, we've got plenty of that, haven't we, Dibber?'

Dibber was a bit slow picking up his cue. 'We do?'

'On the ship,' said Glitz desperately. 'On the ship, Dibber.'

'Oh, black light,' said Dibber. 'Yeah, we got so much of that sometimes you can hardly see.'

'There is black light on your ship?' said Drathro eagerly.

Glitz's story was patently unconvincing, yet the robot grasped at it like a sick man promised a miracle cure. He

118

wanted, needed to believe them.

'As my friend says,' said Dibber smoothly, 'we've got more black light than we know what to do with. So what I suggest is, you come with us and we'll, er, fix you up.'

'Why?' asked Drathro, suddenly suspicious.

'Well, I hate to see a good-looking robot like you go to waste,' said Glitz. 'Tell you what else we can do for you. We can drop you off in the Constellation of Andromeda. How about that?'

'It is possible?' asked Drathro eagerly.

Not only life, but a return home, thought the Doctor. Glitz was quite a con man when he got going. Now for the sting.

'Of course,' said Glitz casually, 'you'd have to bring all the secrets. They'd expect that. You'll have to bring them back.'

'How far is your ship?' asked Drathro.

'Oh, right outside really,' said Glitz vaguely. 'No distance at all.'

'I could function for a short distance.'

'Of course you could,' said Glitz encouragingly.

'I accept your offer,' said Drathro. 'I will fetch the secrets.'

He pointed to Glitz's gun. 'Take that, and tie these others up.'

The robot disappeared into a small inner chamber.

'Well done,' said the Doctor and headed for the black-light console.

Dibber barred his way, laser-gun in hand. 'Sorry, Doc. You heard what he said.'

By the time the robot emerged with a flat metal case in

its metal hand, Peri and Merdeen were securely bound, and Glitz was just finishing lashing the Doctor to a nearby console.

'Don't be a fool,' said the Doctor.

'Slip knot, Doctor,' whispered Glitz. 'Best I can do for you!'

'Strange how low cunning succeeds where intelligence fails,' said the Doctor.

'Don't knock low cunning, Doc,' said Glitz. 'You're still here, aren't you?'

He turned to look greedily at the case in the robot's hand. 'Oh that's it, is it, the secrets? My word there should be a nice lot in there. All on micro dots, no doubt . . . Come along then Dibber, open the door for the Immortal!'

No sooner were the unlikley trio out of the door than the Doctor had slipped his bonds and was releasing Peri and Merdeen.

'Quickly, you've both got to help me. There's a three-stage cut out. I've got to try and shut the machine down.'

'Will that prevent an explosion?' gasped Peri.

The Doctor shook his head. 'All I can hope to do now is contain it.'

By now all three were at the black-light console. The Doctor was making complex adjustments to the controls. The console was vibrating and smoking, almost too hot to touch.

'Peri, you press that row of buttons in front of you!' ordered the Doctor.

Peri looked down. 'Which ones?'

'All of them! Merdeen flick up all the switches with red neons on them.'

Merdeen looked bewildered. 'Red what?'

'Show him, Peri!'

'How much time do we have?' asked Peri.

'Not a lot!' The Doctor was heaving at a lever on the back of the console. 'This thing hasn't been moved in centuries...'

Between them Peri and Merdeen completed their tasks.

'Now what?' asked Peri.

'Get out of here, both of you!'

'What about you, Doctor?'

'Just go. Merdeen, take her out.'

As Merdeen dragged the protesting Peri away, the Doctor heaved the massive lever across at last, adjusted more controls.

The machine was making a strange howling noise. 'Oh dear,' said the Doctor. 'Well, I did my best. I only hope its enough.'

As he turned and dashed out of the control room, it exploded in smoke and flame behind him...

14

End and Beginning

Still wiping the green slime from his face, Balazar was
moving cautiously towards the Castle. The force of the
explosion in the control room knocked him off his feet.

Dibber and Glitz had escorted the staggering robot as far
as the bottom of the steep metal steps. It was weakening
all the time and they were wondering how soon they
could risk getting the metal case away from it and
heading for their ship.

They heard the thunder of the explosion. The robot
staggered and the suddenly began to heat up, giving out a
strange howling sound. Soon it was radiating heat, and
glowing cherry red.

'Look out,' yelled Dibber. 'It's blowing up!'

Dibber and Glitz dived for shelter.

There was a kind of internal explosion and the robot
seemed to collapse inward upon itself. Soon the glow
faded and there was nothing left but a long puddle of
molten metal. Dibber got up and moved to examine it.

Glitz, who had rolled himself into a ball in the corner,
unwound himself and looked up. 'Is it finished?'

Dibber nodded sadly. 'You're not going to like this,
Mr Glitz,' he said lugubriously.

'The robot's finished, and the secrets are finished as well.'

Glitz jumped up. 'What?'

The exploding robot had fused the metal case into a misshapen lump, welded to the remains of the robot's body.

'Still, there's this,' said Dibber casually.

He took a small shiny lump of metal from his pocket.

'And what's that?'

'A piece of black-light convertor aerial,' said Dibber. 'I picked it up when I blew the thing up. Pure siligtone that is.'

'The hardest known metal in the galaxy,' said Glitz.

Dibber nodded. 'And the most expensive. What's more, there's got to be a couple of tons of the stuff in that aerial.'

'I am way ahead of you, my son,' said Glitz. 'You know, we could clean up very nicely on this job – and have a tasty little kitty for the next venture...'

Dibber set off up the stairs.

Glitz paused for a moment looking after him. He'd just been struck by a very worrying thought.

Suppose it was Dibber who was the brainy one after all?

Humker and Tandrell reached the surface at last. They stood looking out of the doorway and something clear and cool came in to meet them, ruffling their hair.

'Fresh air,' said Humker. 'What a wonderful smell.'

Tandrell breathed deeply. For a moment he seemed to be about to produce his usual contrary reaction, and then he smiled.

'Do you know something? You're right. Absolutely right!'

In a tunnel not far from the wrecked castle, the Doctor, covered in dust and grime ran into Balazar, who was as dirty and dusty as the Doctor, was, with an undercoat of green slime as well.

'And still the lobster held on!' said the Doctor cheerfully. 'You're in a worse mess than I am!'

'Are Merdeen and Peri safe, Doctor?'

The Doctor turned and saw two figures running towards them. 'You can ask them yourself, Balazar.'

'Balazar!' shouted Merdeen joyfully, and the two friends ran to greet one another.

Peri marched up to the Doctor and said reproachfully, 'I wish you wouldn't keep frightening me like this!'

'I told you to get out of here,' said the Doctor sternly.

'Please, don't start,' said Peri wearily. 'I'm too tired and too scared to cope.'

'All right, all right,' said the Doctor gently, and put a consoling arm around her shoulders.

'This seems to be the end, Doctor,' said Balazar. 'As it is written in the Books.'

'No, no, Balazar. For you this is the beginning. Chapter One, Paragraph One, as they say. Take your people up on the surface, where they belong.'

'Yes,' said Balazar enthusiastically. 'Perhaps we shall at last find the habitat of the Canadian Goose!'

'Perhaps,' said the Doctor gently. He wiped a bit of green gunk from Balazar's forehead and tasted it cautiously. 'I think dinner's on him!' The Doctor shook Merdeen warmly by the hand. 'Farewell, my loquacious friend!' He looked down at Peri. 'Right, let's get back to the TARDIS.'

He led her briskly away.

Suddenly Peri stopped. 'It's the other way, Doctor.'

'What is?'

'The TARDIS.'

'That's right, it's this way,' agreed the Doctor, instantly changing direction. 'Yes, this way!'

They walked back past the bemused Merdeen and Balazar. 'Farewell!' called the Doctor again – and set off again this time in the right direction.

'There are still one or two questions to be answered of course,' said the Doctor as they moved away. 'Like, who moved this planet two light years off its original course? And what was in that box that Glitz and Dibber were so interested in . . .?'

They heard Balazar's voice calling from behind them. 'Goodbye, old one,' he called. 'Thank you for all your help!'

Peri giggled. 'Old one! Hey that's cute!'

'I always knew there was an evil streak in you,' said the Doctor indignantly. 'Old one, indeed! Come on . . .'

The Doctor led Peri away . . .

. . . and sat back watching himself do it on the Courtroom screen. He leaned back smugly, hands behind his head. 'Well, that's one up to me, I think,' he said modestly. 'There can't be many people who can literally claim to have saved the Universe.' The Doctor rose. 'Well, if that's all the muck you can rake up—'

'Sit down,' said the Valeyard sharply. 'Smugness does not become you, Doctor.'

'That is an irrelevant observation.' He turned to the Inquisitor. 'I take it that it is now my turn to present the case for the defense?'

'In due course, Doctor.'

'But that's not fair! Look, I wish it put on record that my involvement in the affairs of that planet resulted in the freeing of Drathro's underground slaves.'

The Inquisitor inclined her head. 'That has been noted.'

'And despite the fact that evidence has been withheld, my presence there was most specifically requested.'

'You showed little reluctance in complying with the request,' observed the Valeyard acidly.

'Well, lives were at stake.'

'Lives were lost – and lost because of your meddling, Doctor.'

'I deny that,' said the Doctor hotly. 'Without my help, an entire civilization might have been wiped out.'

'Without your interference Doctor, there might have been less sacrifice of human life!'

'That was a risk I had to take!'

'Risk,' snarled the Valeyard. 'Risk? Hear how the Doctor condemns himself by his own words!'

'Gentlemen!' the Inquisitor's voice cut off both the Valeyards continuing speech, and the Doctor's intended reply.

'Perhaps you should heed the Valeyard, Doctor,' said the Inquisitor. 'May I suggest that for the time being you have said enough.'

'Said enough?' spluttered the Doctor. 'Said enough? I have a great deal more to say. I wish to demonstrate—'

'Be silent, Doctor,' said the Inquisitor.

Somewhat to his own surprise, the Doctor obeyed.

'You will have your turn when the Valeyard has finished his presentation,' went on the Inquisitor.

The Valeyard bowed low. 'Thank you, My Lady.'

The Doctor sat back in his chair. 'Well, if the rest of his presentation is as riveting as this little epic, you can wake me when he's finished!'

'Finished,' said the Valeyard venomously. 'I've barely started!'

'Well, if only for the sake of your career in the legal profession, I only hope your evidence gets a little better.'

'Better?' sneered the Valeyard. 'Oh yes, much better, Doctor. The most damning is still to come. And when I *have* finished—' The Valeyard's voice rose in a crescendo of anger. 'When I have finished, Doctor, this Court will demand your life!'

The Doctor held the Valeyard's angry stare with his own for a moment then sat back in his chair.

The Doctor loved a good mystery and there were many mysteries here.

There were questions to be answered. Not only those he'd posed to Peri on Ravolox – or Earth, as it seemed to be, but questions about this precious Trial or Inquiry, or whatever it was.

Why was he here – and where was he come to that?

Who was the Valeyard, and why was he so passionate for the Doctor's death?

What part would the enigmatic Inquisitor play? Why had certain evidence been suppressed?

Perhaps his next adventure would reveal the answers . . .

Eyes fixed on the screen, the Doctor sat back, waiting for his next adventure to begin.

He was quite looking forward to it.

THIS OFFER EXCLUSIVE TO

READERS

**Pin up magnificent full colour posters of
DOCTOR WHO**

**Just send £2.50 for the first poster and £1.25
for each additional poster**

TO: PUBLICITY DEPARTMENT *
      W. H. ALLEN & CO PLC
      44 HILL STREET
      LONDON W1X 8LB

Cheques, Postal Orders made payable to WH Allen PLC

POSTER 1 ☐   **POSTER 2** ☐   **POSTER 3** ☐
POSTER 4 ☐   **POSTER 5** ☐

Please allow 28 DAYS for delivery.

I enclose £ _____

CHEQUE NO. _____

ACCESS, VISA CARD NO. _____

Name _____

Address _____

_____

*For Australia, New Zealand, USA and Canada apply to distributors
listed on back cover for details and local price list*